The Pleasure Garden

The trees began to rustle, at first softly and then with increasing violence. The arbours began to shake, vines snapped and leaves fell to the ground. Then out of the low branches and down the sides and backs of the arbours slid and dropped various black creatures, like misshapen fruits: they were children, of supernaturally ragged and filthy appearance. They scuttled along the paths to the dark and silent house, slipped through a door and shuffled into an underground parlour. They grew still as Mrs Bray, proprietress of the Mulberry Garden, entered the cellar.

"And how does my garden grow?" she asked. She took up her pen and began to write as the children began their nightly catechism. In high, monotonous voices they disgorged the secrets they'd heard, the dreams, the lies, the unwitting truths and the tender intimacies their bright little eyes had spied out as they'd lain hidden on the tops of the arbours and stared down through peepholes in the trellises and vines. Finally they came to an end.

"Good night little ones," she said as they finished. "And God bless you, every one!"

Leon Garfield

The Pleasure Garden

Illustrated by Fritz Wegner

LIONS · TRACKS

First published by Penguin Books Ltd 1976
First published in Lions Tracks 1991

Lions Tracks is an imprint of
the Children's Division, part of
HarperCollins Publishers Ltd,
8 Grafton Street, London W1X 3LA

Printed and bound in Great Britain by
William Collins Sons & Co. Ltd, Glasgow

To Ursula

Chapter One

EASTWARD in Clerkenwell lies the Mulberry Pleasure Garden: six acres of leafy walks, colonnades, pavilions and arbours of box, briar and vine, walled in between Rag Street and New Prison Walk. When night falls, the garden opens its eyes; lamps hang glimmering in the trees and scores of moths flap and totter in the shadowy green, imagining themselves star-drunk . . .

> '*Love in her eyes sits playing,*
> *And sheds delicious death . . .*'

That's Orpheus Jones, a sweet Welsh tenor who sells gloves by day in Compton Street and sings each night for his supper and a guinea a week besides. He stands on the balcony of the gilded rotunda near the mulberry tree itself and, accompanied by three fiddles and a flute, sends his voice as far as Corporation Lane:

'*Deli-i-i-ishus death!*' (His flexible roulades drive his imitators to despair.)

'Delicious! That's the word for you!'

That's Major Smith, who comes every Friday night, and occupies arbour number twelve.

'I shouldn't be here with you! Really I shouldn't. I'm doing very wrong, Major Smith. What would your wife say, if she knew?'

And that's Leila Robinson, as lovely as the summer's dark can make her, sitting beside the major, who is a sturdy little man with astonishingly gentle eyes. He sighs:

'My dear, my wife is dead. She was an Indian girl; she passed away while we were still in Bombay.'

'Oh I'm sorry . . . truly sorry.'

'She was beautiful, in that passionate way of the East,' murmurs the major reminiscently, stroking Miss Robinson's wrist. 'We had only been married a month . . .'

'Forgive me!' whispers Leila. 'I didn't know –'

> '*Love on her lips is straying*
> *And warbling in her breath!*'

Orpheus Jones is in fine voice. He sings with closed eyes and exposed teeth, leaning forward like a lover about to bite.

'*Stray-ay-ay-ing* . . .'

'Waiter! Waiter, sir! Bring us a dish of syllabub, there's a dear! Don't you worry, Mr Brown! I'm rich today!'

That's Fanny Bush with her threadbare, skin-and-bone old friend whom she loves to treat, every Friday, to a night out in the garden. As the waiter departs, she presses a coin into old Mr Brown's trembling palm and makes him

8

promise to spend the money wisely, on nourishing food. Her eyes sparkle with pleasure and compassion.

A youngish man, of perhaps twenty-seven or -eight, watches and wonders if the old beggar is the pretty young woman's grandfather. Then he returns to eating his cheese-cake, for which he has an undeniable weakness. He is the Reverend Martin Young, Vicar of St James's and Justice of the Peace, to boot.

> *'Love on her breast sits panting*
> *And swells with soft desire!'*

Orpheus Jones flings out his arms and blindly embraces the garden. A wood pigeon coos and from somewhere the last nightingale in Clerkenwell begins to sing. Everywhere in the arbours and the shady places that abound, hands are clasped, lips meet, eyes wink and glimmer and then go out. Discreetly, like benevolent spirits, waiters clink away empty glasses ... and discreetly forget to bring change.

A man, ugly as sin (God knows why he comes, for to the ugly the garden is torment!), looks wistfully towards the nooks and bowers, glimpses the frill of a disturbed petti-coat, and suffers the tortures of the damned.

> *'No grace, no charm is wanting,*
> *To set the heart on fire!'*

Tom Hastey and his Lucy suit their actions to the song's words. Of all the Friday-nighters, they are the best be-loved. Their hearts are on fire, all right, and Tom swears, as usual, that he's about to make his fortune and they'll live happily ever after; and Lucy believes him, while keeping a sharp eye out for her guardian aunt who's at the raffling-booth, determined to win, this time, a silver and enamel watch ...

9

At eleven o'clock by the bell of St James's, Orpheus Jones bows and retires to his supper, while the band plays on till the garden closes, half an hour after midnight. The booths in the colonnades give up trading and pack away their wares. Lucy's guardian aunt leaves the raffling-shop, having won a paper fan, and peevishly calls to her charge; and the twelve arbours disgorge their contents in the shape of lovers old and young, who wend their linked ways along the winding walks that lead to the gate.

Here the garden's secular arm, in the shape of a party of muscular servants armed with torches and cudgels and in green livery, awaits such solitary females as need escorting through the terrors of the night. Slowly and laughingly, with promises and assignations for the Friday to come, the revellers go out of the pleasure garden, out into the black garden of pain.

*

The Mulberry Garden was given up to darkness and quiet. The three fiddles, the flute and the singer had gone home; the waiters, stalking on tiptoes like shabby crows with napkins and corns, had poked and pried in the arbours and under the tables for valuables left behind, and then, with long snuffers, put out the lanterns in the trees.

A great stillness lay over the garden; such a stillness that the imagination might have heard the motion of a spider or the scream of a fly.

Suddenly there came the sound of a bell – a small, frail ringing: once, twice, three times . . .

The trees began to rustle, at first softly and then with increasing violence. Again the bell rang. The arbours began to shake, vines snapped and leaves fell to the ground. For a moment it seemed that the garden was in the grip of the ghosts of dead lovers, called up by the bell to partake of the warmth left by the living. Indeed, the garden was reputed to be haunted . . .

Then this invisible violence died as mysteriously as it had sprung up; and out of the low branches and down the sides and backs of the arbours slid and dropped various black creatures, like misshapen fruits.

Perhaps a dozen, in all, made up this eerie windfall. Silently they gestured to each other before scuttling along the paths to the dark and silent house that adjoined the gate.

One by one they slipped through a back door and began to descend a flight of stone steps. The rattle of feet and the noise of panting suggested that a small-sized hailstorm had got inside the house and panicked.

A door opened and light streamed out. The storm abated and shuffled into an underground parlour that was furnished with a table, two chairs and several stout benches, like a magistrate's court. The light came from a solitary lantern on the table that jumped and flinched as the storm dispersed itself and sat upon the benches. Then the flame grew steady . . .

The dark creatures, the windfall from the arbours, turned out to be children, human children of supernaturally ragged and filthy appearance. Several of them exhibited cuts and scratches from thorns and broken branches, and it seemed that they'd bled not blood but dirt, that they were dirt all through, that their very bones were grubby and the marrow in them was as black as sin. Only their eyes, the windows of their souls, were bright and gleeful, being composed of a substance that even dirt shrank from . . .

'Where's Briskitt?'

The voice, sharp as a pin, came from behind the lamp where a long, thin man in black appeared to be folded rather than seated in one of the chairs. Had he not spoken, there might have been nothing but dark upholstery on the chair . . .

'Briskitt! Briskitt!'

''Ere I am, Dr Dormann, sir! Jus' come!' The latecomer appeared. He was a scrawny infant with a diminutive face, like screwed-up paper. As was his invariable habit, he was full of breathless excuses and apologies.

'Couldn't 'elp bein' late! Got caught up in that there bleedin' vine again!'

He offered in evidence a tear in the remnant of his sleeve, and enlarged it. Dr Dormann leaned forward till he seemed all face, pale and luminous.

'Vines don't bleed, Briskitt,' he said with gentle reproach. 'They hang. You must bear that in mind. We don't want the same to happen to you, do we?'

There was the merest trace of an accent in the doctor's speech; but it was so slight that no one could have told where he came from. An Englishman might have said Scotland; a Scotsman might have said Ireland; and an Irishman might have made a guess at Germany.

Briskitt, suitably admonished, hung his head and went to join his colleagues with a perfectly outrageous grin the doctor was unable to see.

At last, when Briskitt had settled himself beside a particular friend, Dr Dormann flashed his teeth – which were new – and again rang the small brass bell that had summoned the children from the trees. As he did so, he rose, by a process of unfolding, and gestured, with appallingly white hands, for the company to follow his example.

A moment later there was a sound of heavy footsteps, a rustling, and a clinking of glass. The children grew still and Mrs Bray, followed by a servant bearing a tray of mulberry cordial, entered the cellar. Dr Dormann bowed . . .

Mrs Bray was the proprietress of the Mulberry Garden. According to the best judges, she was the fattest woman in London and was said to have topped four and twenty stone on a butcher's scale in Smithfield; though how and when she had ever been persuaded into such a situation defied all conjecture.

Although a widow for seven years, she still wore black, which lent her bulk a certain mystery; sometimes it was hard to see where she ended and the night began. Dr Dormann, standing beside her, looked thinner than ever; really no more than a mere slice of a man who might have come off Mrs Bray in a carelessly slammed door.

'All present, Dr D.?' asked the lady, beaming kindly.

Eagerly Dr Dormann flashed his teeth again; and Mrs Bray, seating herself with infinite care, nodded to her servant to distribute the mulberry cordial which had been measured out into old beer bottles.

'For what we are about to receive?' inquired Mrs Bray.

'May the Lord make us truly grateful!' answered the children; and without more ado set about swigging down the dark drink, upending the bottles and regulating the flow by inserting their narrow, pointed tongues. They resembled, in the twitching, jumping lantern-light, mischievous imps who had just come out of the bottles and were partly stuck.

None of them was much above ten years old, nor higher than Mrs Bray's double-barrelled breast. She might have picked up any two of them without embarrassment, and walked off with them, struggle as they might.

Indulgently the huge lady watched the curious scene, while forming, perhaps, the most curious part of it herself. Presently Dr Dormann rang the bell, to which the children seemed to have been rigorously trained. At once they desisted from the bottles and, emptying the dregs over the nearest head or down a convenient neck, returned to their benches. As they sat before Mrs Bray and Dr Dormann in an orderly fashion, they might have been a Sunday School, only it was Friday night; and the great ledger that Dr Dormann now opened and laid before his mistress was not, by any stretch of the imagination, a Bible.

Mrs Bray drew the lamp towards her and put on a pair of spectacles which dwindled to dewdrops in her huge face.

'And how does my garden grow?' she asked with a burst of playfulness.

'With silver bells and cockleshells and pretty maids all in a row!' answered the children, dutifully.

'One, two, buckle my shoe!' cried Mrs Bray, clapping her hands.

Two scraps of animated mud and earth came forward and fidgeted just outside the circle of lamplight.

'Well? Well? Buckle my shoe!'

She took up a pen and began to write, in large, laborious letters, as One and Two began upon the nightly catechism.

'I heard . . .'

'I saw . . .'

'I heard . . .'

'I saw . . .'

In high, monotonous voices the children disgorged the secrets they'd heard, the dreams, the lies, the unwitting truths and the tender intimacies their bright little eyes had spied out as they'd lain hidden on the tops of the arbours and stared down through peep-holes in the trellises and vines.

Mrs Bray listened and wrote, listened and wrote, pausing only to push up her spectacles which slipped down her short, broad nose. At last the children ceased and Mrs Bray nodded to Dr Dormann who gave them each a sixpence for their pains. She turned the page of the ledger.

'Three and four, knock on my door!'

One and Two bobbed and retired, giving way to Three and Four.

'Well, little ones? Knock on my door!'

Three and Four knocked to great advantage ... and when they were done, why, there was a sixpence each for Three and Four! Then came Five and Six, who picked up sticks; and Seven and Eight, who laid them straight ...

'Nine and Ten, a big fat hen!' cried Mrs Bray, happily. 'Well, little ones? And what have you got for your big fat hen?'

They had a great deal, and Mrs Bray, no fluent penwoman, had to write long and hard in her ledger, which must have contained all the dreams and little sins in the world.

Last to speak was Briskitt, the unseen genius of arbour number twelve, where Major Smith and Leila Robinson had –

'Dig and delve,' urged Mrs Bray. 'Dig and delve!'

'They was wrapped up closer'n a bundle of washin', marm! I never seed sich goin's-on; nor comin's-off, neither!' said Briskitt, concluding a tale of such lecherous delights that the very cellar walls seemed to blush at it.

Briskitt took his sixpence, bowed neatly and, with his companion, went back to his place. Mrs Bray closed the ledger with a soft bang. She stood up and shook out her dress, and a strong smell of sandalwood perfume, which she always wore, was wafted across the room.

'Good night, little ones,' she said, taking off her spectacles and wiping her eyes. 'And God bless you, every one!'

She moved to stand by the cellar door and, as each child

went past her, she bent to kiss it on its earthy brow. Three of these night children, among whom was Briskitt, lodged in the stables; the others lived with their natural mothers who were engaged in the forced occupation of beating hemp in nearby Bridewell Gaol.

'Dr D.!'

Dr Dormann looked up. He had reopened the ledger, and had been studying it while the children had been departing. Mrs Bray moved to his side and peered down at the opened page. Nothing was written on it but a name at the top. Martin Young.

Gently Mrs Bray shook her head.

'Not that one, Dr D. Never that one.'

'Why not?'

'I told you before. I had a dream about this page. There was blood on it.'

'Whose blood?'

'I don't know. It might have been yours, Dr D.'

She pushed Dr Dormann aside and turned the ledger's pages until she came to the sworn affidavit for arbour number twelve.

'Now this one, Dr D. This is more in our line.'

Obediently Dr Dormann leaned forward and examined the evidence that related to no less than three Fridays in succession. Major Smith's page was full.

'Tomorrow, Dr D. See to it tomorrow.'

She closed the book with finality, locking the clasp with a small key that she kept on a chain that descended into her bosom. Dr Dormann's eyes lingered on the great volume that was bound in calf and tooled with the gilded replica of a mulberry tree.

'I know what you're thinking, Dr D. But remember, I dreamed of blood.'

Chapter Two

DR DORMANN also had dreams; but they were not of blood. Perhaps they were not so much dreams as peculiarly intense reveries that overcame him even when he was walking the streets. He did not, to his knowledge, dream when he was asleep. Indeed, sleep and its oblivion frightened him so much that he would actually lie awake for hours, trembling at the thought of its inevitability.

When he fell into one of these reveries, to which he was increasingly subject and which were usually heralded by a sense of coldness, his expression would become almost rapt in its inwardness. On several occasions he had been taken for a blind man or even some sort of religious fanatic. This latter impression was reinforced by his habit of wearing Geneva bands – those limp white ribbons that hang, like folded wings, below a clergyman's chin.

But Dr Dormann was not a doctor of divinity. In fact, no one really knew from what branch of learning his doctorate had been plucked. It might have been law, it might have been physic, it might have been philosophy; it might even have been from a branch of the mulberry tree itself.

Where had he come from? A debtor's prison. Mrs Bray had found him, bought his liberty and given him employment. 'I need a man,' she'd said, 'to go about for me.'

And before that? A small business that had failed. And before that? A youth and childhood lost somewhere, far, far away in some ancient, crazy town where casements leaned across streets like gossiping monsters; a town of ghosts and bloodied doorposts . . .

Sometimes he felt his life stretched back for centuries ... lonely, empty, rootless. He grimaced wryly; even his teeth lacked roots.

He was walking up Ludgate Hill and, despite the warmth of the August morning, he began to shiver. Desperately he tried to ward off the attack that he felt to be imminent. He was out upon Mrs Bray's business; nothing must be allowed to interfere with it. The huge woman commanded his whole loyalty, and, some would have said, his soul itself. Also his attacks had become, lately, almost nightmarish ...

He paused to recover himself and then walked on with a firmness of step that denoted the danger was past. At length he reached his destination, a respectable-looking woollen draper's with the name A. Woodcock displayed on a sign above the door. He gazed thoughtfully in the window as if meditating a purchase, when a neatly dressed youth emerged from the shop and actually seized him by the sleeve as if to prevent him changing his mind.

'You're in luck, sir!' confided this youth energetically. 'It's just come in! Black worsted such as you've never laid eyes on! Fifteen shillin's the yard; and I can tell you, the weavers would 'ave our guts for garters if they knew we was sellin' it that cheap! Come right on inside, sir, an' be measured. I tell you, we're expectin' such a rush once it gets about that Sodom an' Tomarrah'll be nothin' on it ... beggin' Your Reverence's pardon! But I'm 'appy to tell you, sir,' pattered on the youth, drawing his captive irresistibly inside the shop, 'that we make special terms for gentlemen of the cloth like yourself. It's on account of us bein' so near the cathedral, y'know. The Harchbishop of Canterbury hoften drops in ...'

Without either stopping or releasing his customer, the youth dexterously shut the door behind him with his foot, and two girls, who'd been perched on rolls of cloth, giggled and fled, calling:

'Pa! Pa! Shop!'

A moment later, the woollen draper himself came forward, bowing from the neck and rubbing his hands. He was a sturdy little man with astonishingly gentle eyes.

Now here was a remarkable thing. Mr A. Woodcock, woollen draper of Ludgate Hill, with large wife and oppressive daughters, was identical in every respect to Major Smith, the romantic, childless widower from Bombay, who had consoled himself so passionately on Leila Robinson's breast in the Mulberry Garden, and filled up a whole page in the ledger.

'Ah! Mr Woodcock, sir!' said the youth, absolutely determined to make a go of things. 'This Rev. gent's come in about our new line. The one we calls the Harchbishop's choice.'

'*Good* morning, sir. *Good* morning!' said the draper, sincerely.

He signed to the youth to deliver up the gentleman into his own more experienced hands, from which he appeared to be removing the last traces of some invisible glue.

Instantly, as if Dr Dormann's sleeve had been red hot, the youth relinquished his hold and, bowing his way out backwards, vanished into the rear of the shop where he was heard to stumble and provoke a muffled outburst of female mirth.

The draper looked deprecating.

'Your daughters?' asked Dr Dormann with a mild surprise that suggested admiration.

The draper did not contest the relationship.

'Delightful young ladies. I congratulate you.'

'Very kind of you to say so. I've another girl,' went on

19

Mr Woodcock, with moderate enthusiasm, 'upstairs with her mother.'

'A fine family,' said Dr Dormann, smiling.

'Devoted,' said the draper, courteously echoing his customer's smile.

'You are to be envied,' said Dr Dormann, looking round the humdrum shop.

'I count my blessings, sir.'

'The best arithmetic!'

The draper laughed appreciatively and removed another skin of glue from his hands. 'Wonderful weather we're having,' he said intelligently.

'Quite a Bombay summer,' said Dr Dormann.

'Bombay? Oh! Yes! I see what you mean! Indian. An Indian summer indeed!' A bead of perspiration began to trickle down the side of the draper's nose, as if in visible confirmation of the heat.

'I brung the Harchbishop's choice and one or two other things what might be of hinterest!' panted several rolls of black cloth, supported on spindly legs that had just staggered in from the back of the shop.

'And now, sir,' said the draper, steadying the apparition, which threatened to collapse, 'did you have in mind a suit, or a gown? Of course, if you should decide on both, then we can come down quite nicely in your favour.'

'Neither, Mr – er – Woodstock.'

'I beg your pardon, sir?'

'I said, neither. Neither a suit nor a gown.'

'Ah! You want breeches, then! Or maybe a coat?'

'You mistake me, Mr – er – Woodcock. I did not come in to buy. Your apprentice gave me no chance to explain myself . . .'

A sound of indignation came from behind the rolls of cloth.

'If you did not come to buy, sir, what, might I ask, is the purpose of your visit?'

'Charity, Mr Woodcock. I called on a matter of charity.'

Slowly, the rolls of cloth began to depart. The draper watched them, his face reddening with anger. He turned back to Dr Dormann.

'Really, sir! This is a place of business! In my opinion – for what it's worth – you are going about things very . . . very . . .' He sought for a word, and then, staring pointedly at Dr Dormann's black suit, came out with: 'Shabbily. Very shabbily indeed. How would you like it, sir,' he went on with mounting irritation, 'if I was to come into your church and set about peddling my cloth? I'll tell you what. You wouldn't like it at all. You would tell me to keep to my own place of business. And you'd be right. So now I say to you, sir, keep your begging for charity inside your church where it belongs. Good day to you, sir.'

Mr Woodcock opened his shop door and stood staring rigidly in front of him.

'It is a worthy cause,' said Dr Dormann mildly.

'I'm sorry to hear it. That is, I mean, I'm glad the cause is worthy, but I am sorry I cannot assist. I have enough mouths to feed as it is. Good *day*,' he concluded, changing the emphasis from *good* to *day*, as if to indicate that the relationship between them had deteriorated.

'A military man in reduced circumstances,' pursued Dr Dormann who had approached the door but showed no sign of going through it.

'Let him do an honest day's work, then!'

'A widower, Mr – er – Woodcock,' said Dr Dormann, quietly. 'Wife died in Bombay. Only married a month. Sad case. Childless. Name of Smith. Major Smith.'

The door swung shut. There was silence in the shop, broken only by the sound of harsh, irregular breathing.

The draper had gone very white. His eyes were bulging and rolling from side to side. It was impossible to say whether anger or fear was getting the upper hand. Dr Dormann remained as close to the door as he could. One never knew how these little visits he undertook for Mrs Bray would end up. Once he'd actually been struck; and several times he'd only owed his safety to a surprising turn of speed.

'Major Smith –'

'I – I've never heard of him!' muttered the wretched draper, glaring at the doctor and then up to the ceiling beyond which was his unsuspecting wife and third daughter. He could not, for the life of him, imagine how the blow had fallen or how he'd been betrayed. His brain was overwhelmed with horrible possibilities. He suspected his apprentice, his daughters and every single person he knew! And worst of all, he suspected Leila Robinson . . .

'Fifty pounds would save him,' breathed Dr Dormann, getting ready to make a bolt for it if things should go badly.

'I – I deny everything!' moaned the draper, with a burst of hysterical defiance.

'Fifty pounds and you don't need to,' said Dr Dormann. If the man had been going to attack him, he would have done so by now.

Mr Woodcock was sweating like a pig. His whole life hung in the balance. He could think of nothing beyond extricating himself from the terrible situation that had overwhelmed him. And out of a cruelly clear sky!

'Ch-charity, you said?'

'Charity, I said.'

'And fifty pounds would save . . . would help – Major Smith?'

'Fifty pounds and he wouldn't have another care in the world. And after all,' went on Dr Dormann, with a sudden smile of compassion, 'fifty pounds is not very much to save a man from . . . ruin.'

'Fifty pounds . . . fifty pounds. Yes; if you put it that way . . . But, oh my God! How did you know? Who was it? Will you tell me that? Was it *her*? Don't say it was Miss Robinson? Did she tell you? But how could she! She doesn't know! She must never know! Promise me that!'

'Set your mind at rest, Mr Woodcock. The lady you mentioned will know no more than you wish her to. The money, after all, is to save Major Smith, and whatever is his.'

The draper passed a hand across his brow. He was actually crying with relief. Curiously enough, his tears were not for the saving of his family, but for Leila Robinson. Though their relationship had been of brief duration, it had become immensely precious to him. Somehow his existence as the military Bombay widower was even more important than his life as a woollen draper in Ludgate Hill. There were times, very private times, when he dreamed of going away with Miss Robinson for ever. She renewed him; when he was with her he felt all the panting excitement he'd not known since he was a boy. Fifty pounds was very little to preserve it.

And in addition to that, he went on, arguing inside his head as if there was someone there who still needed convincing, he would be sparing his wife a singularly wounding discovery. Fifty pounds was really a trifle to that! It wouldn't be the unfaithfulness she'd be injured by, but the fact that he'd represented himself as childless and bereaved; that, in effect, he'd wished her and her children dead . . . or never to have lived at all; that in the deepest part of his heart he'd always yearned for a woman more beautiful, more mysterious and more abandoned than the one he'd got.

All these frantic and contradictory thoughts were reflected in the draper's face, which Dr Dormann watched with a touch of weariness.

'I'll get the – the money now!'

Dr Dormann nodded.

'Will you – will you take a bank-note?'

'Yes.'

'Thank you – thank you! That's very good of you.'

The draper hastened from the shop and returned holding out the money. Dr Dormann took it and, in exchange, gave the draper a pewter medallion of about the size of a large coin. A mulberry tree was engraved on it.

'What is it?'

'It is ... your season ticket, Mr Woodcock. For the garden, you understand.' The draper stared down at the medallion ... and then felt an inexplicable rush of warmth and gratitude to the lean, intense man in black who had the indefinable air of some religion about him. Carefully he put the medallion, which was the visible confirmation of the bargain, into his pocket. He smiled timidly at Dr Dormann, and held out his hand. Warmly Dr Dormann shook it, and, for a moment, there was a most extraordinary friendship between the two men ... a profound intimacy as of confessor and sinner ... It was almost a moment of exaltation.

'I think you have been very wise, Mr Woodcock.'

'I had no choice, sir.'

'True. No real choice.'

'Miss Robinson will never find out?'

'The Mulberry Garden keeps faith. You'll find that it is quite a place of faith.'

'And are there many ... of the faithful in it, sir?'

'Put such thoughts out of your mind, my friend. Content yourself with the garden and don't look to the

24

Tree of Knowledge. Be satisfied with the Tree of Life.'

The draper nodded and smiled quite happily. Now that the matter was settled, it was noticeable that he had become quite boyish and relaxed, while Dr Dormann, on the other hand, had grown almost stern and was showing a marked inclination to lift the conversation onto a metaphysical or allegorical plane.

'Don't mind me,' said the draper lightly. 'I was only being curious.'

'Curiosity cost us all the Garden of Eden, my friend. Take care that it doesn't cost you the Mulberry Garden.'

'I don't know what we should do without you, Dr D.', said Mrs Bray, when Dr Dormann returned and handed her the bank-note. She was in her upstairs parlour with curtains drawn against the afternoon light as she had weak eyes that became inflamed in the sun.

Dr Dormann smiled gratefully for the praise, even though the 'we' was painful to him.

Although the management of the garden was left largely to him, the genius behind it all was that of Mr Bray. The idea of recruiting the children to spy among the branches had been Mr Bray's, his widow always declared, even though he never lived to see his dream come true. 'And surely,' she added, 'they're better off in the natural green than running about in the streets and getting run down and killed?' Even the idea of taking on such a helper as Dr Dormann, she liked to say without realizing the pain she was inflicting, had been in Mr Bray's mind as he'd lain dying.

No one at present employed in the garden could remember Mr Bray. He had been dead for seven years; and there was a rumour, not contradicted by his widow, that he was buried in the shade of the mulberry tree itself.

'So you see,' said Mrs Bray, 'while his poor body feeds our roots, his spirit feeds everything else. I can always feel him about.'

Whether or not she really believed his ghost walked the garden was impossible to say; her simplicity and credulity were on the massive scale. But the children believed it; and whenever Mrs Bray had occasion to say, 'Mr Bray's watching you. *He* knows . . .', they became as little angels of industry and obedience in the garden's leafy sky.

'You'd best go down and enter it up in the ledger, Dr D.,' said Mrs Bray, unfastening the key from its chain and handing it to her assistant. 'It looks like we might get the lake finished this season after all.'

The lake in question was another of Mr Bray's dreams and was, at present, a large muddy pit in the northern end of the garden. It was to be paved with water-lilies and filled with swans and God knew what else besides.

'Another couple of Major Smiths, eh?' chuckled Mrs Bray. She lifted up her skirt – inadvertently displaying a pair of huge silken legs – and stowed the bank-note in a money-belt she kept round her waist.

Dr Dormann bowed and went down to the cellar. He unlocked the ledger and duly receipted the page of Major Smith. Then he turned, with a feeling of almost dread to the spotless page of the priest-magistrate: Martin Young.

He began to feel cold. At first he thought it was only the chill of the stone cellar; then he realized, too late, that the attack he had warded off earlier was returning. This time he was unable to prevent it.

He sat down, shaking all over. His eyes seemed to turn in on themselves and he had to press his hands to his jaw to prevent his teeth from jumping out.

As always, he was sitting in the pit of an enormous theatre. He was utterly alone; there was not another soul in either the boxes or the gallery. There was a play in progress on the stage. It was a stupid, tedious affair, full of bad jokes and endless, senseless cudgellings such as are common in puppet shows. The actors were all wearing masks, crudely painted paper masks such as children tie on effigies for a bonfire. As he watched, he couldn't help feeling how absurd it all was – this dreadful, extravagant performance – for an audience of one! So he began to laugh. He couldn't stop. He laughed and laughed till the tears ran down his cheeks; and when he tried to wipe them away, he found that he, too, was masked. Angrily he attempted to take it off; he wanted desperately to see what mask it was he was wearing; but it was glued on and tore his skin.

Suddenly he noticed that all the actors had lined up in front of the footlights and were watching him. He felt horribly ashamed and embarrassed.

'Masks off! Masks off!' shouted a voice that he knew to be Martin Young's, though he could not see him anywhere. 'It's on the stroke of doomsday!'

Then everyone ripped off their paper faces, leaving blood and bones to the open view. This was the worst moment of all, because he knew that he must take off his own mask, and, with it, his face.

'I warned you about that page, Dr D.,' said Mrs Bray, who had come down to the cellar to see what was keeping her assistant. 'You've had one of your turns again, haven't you?'

He nodded. 'It's over now, ma'am.'

'I told you I dreamed of blood. Look!'

During his seizure, Dr Dormann must have bitten his tongue and dribbled a little. There were several small spots of blood on the blank page.

Chapter Three

THERE are certain individuals who, either because of a particular cast of features, or some deeper, more mysterious quality, convey so decided an impression of good or evil that neither their words, deeds or inward feelings – however contradictory – are capable of effacing. Such an individual was Martin Young, who found himself – sometimes shamefacedly – revered far beyond what he knew to be his just deserts.

The second son of a well-to-do country gentleman, his earliest education had been left to a deeply religious Scottish nurse, who, strongly impressed by his gentle and slightly unearthly charm, conceived the gloomy notion that he was not long for this world. Accordingly she filled his infant head with superstitious tales of martyrs and saints, so that, when the melancholy time came, 'the little bairn might go bonnily to his gude Father in Heaven'.

However, instead of going to heaven, the child stayed firmly on the earth and had nightmares about being broken on the family carriage wheel or being roasted as a heretic on the kitchen spit. Then, when he was nine – and certainly old enough to know better – he 'borrowed' a velvet cloak belonging to his mother and, following the example of his namesake, St Martin – whose story he had taken to heart – he cut it in two and gave half to a beggar he had seen at the gate.

He bore his punishment meekly enough; but, far from showing signs of contrition, when he was released from confinement, he took another leaf from St Martin's book and attempted to convert his mother to Christianity. Mrs Young, a brisk, sensibly devout lady, was outraged at being piped at by her spiritual child. He was soundly thrashed, the nurse dismissed and his education put in more orthodox hands.

But it made no difference. Though he attempted no further acts of saintliness, and indulged in the sinful propensities of any growing boy, there was always about him an uncanny air of gentleness and unassailable goodness. He had only to walk into a room of strangers and at once a sense of peace and comfort prevailed. He did not, by any means, possess the power of healing, yet his presence in a sickroom really did communicate an extraordinary confidence to the sufferer. When his own father lay dying, of a painful, and foul-smelling, abdominal disorder, the coming of Martin to the bedside (fresh, it must be admitted, from some shameful escapade) seemed to cast out the devil of pain and allow the old gentleman to pass away in dignity.

He took Holy Orders, even though he felt himself un-suited to the church; he was a younger son and there was little else open to him. He obtained the living of St James's in Clerkenwell and attempted, heart and soul, to live up to the bright spirit that seemed to radiate from him, almost against his will. After two years, he undertook the commission of the peace, becoming a clerical justice, or priest-magistrate, and was able to combine his two duties, despite their apparent contradiction. By the time he was twenty-eight, he was revered in the parish, where he had worked unceasingly, even as an artist serves his talent by improving his craft. It was impossible for him not to feel that the mysterious quality he had was a talent lodged with him by God and which he must serve, even though it sometimes went against the grain.

His follies and shortcomings – of which he was always drawing up mental lists with the honest intention of over-coming them, one by one – were: personal vanity, a more than pastoral interest in pretty parishioners, a strong streak of the theatrical that had occasioned his bishop to reproach him with 'too much pulpit effort, Young'; and a childish passion for cheese-cake that he indulged in the Mulberry Garden every Friday night.

On Friday, 16 August, he was more ready than ever to succumb to the relatively harmless delights of the pleasure garden. He had had a bad day and had not recovered from it.

Earlier in the afternoon he had been summoned to Bridewell Gaol – where he acted as chaplain – to attend what was confidently expected to be a deathbed. He had prayed by the dying woman, whom he remembered as an habitual offender against public decency, and had sat beside her, overcoming a natural repugnance and stroking her ice-cold forehead so that whatever power it was that he possessed might enter into her and give her peace. Then, quite suddenly, she'd opened her eyes and, seeing beside her not the priest who was comforting her but the magistrate who'd condemned her, she'd let loose such a torrent of hatred and obscenity that Martin had been shaken to the depths of his soul.

'I think she'll be all right, now,' had said the Governor, escorting the chaplain from the gaol; and thought no more about it. But Martin's ears still burned and his hands were trembling with agitation. He felt sick that the woman's attack had in some way betrayed his own weaknesses and injured the spirit he tried so hard to serve.

He was late in the garden; his usual place was taken by a noisy party of strangers, so he walked on till he found an empty seat. All he wanted was to be left alone and to listen to the music. A waiter came deferentially to his side and took his order for cheese-cake and wine. He went away and Martin closed his eyes and strove to surrender himself to the garden.

'Good evenin', sir. Would you like to buy me a drink?'

With a start he looked up. One of the garden's numerous whores was swaying before him. Her eyes were ringed with lamp-black and her mouth wore a crudely painted smile. But under it all was a young face that somehow looked frightened to death.

'Would you like to, sir?'

The waiter, who'd returned with the cake and wine, glanced curiously at the whore and discreetly at the clergyman. He coughed and hovered away.

Martin picked up his glass; his hands were shaking more violently than ever. He felt everyone in the garden was watching; he was furiously ashamed of being accosted. She had no right. Not wanting to speak, he waved the girl away as if she'd been an insect. It was a stupid, arrogant action, contrary to everything in his nature; he regretted it almost at once.

The girl (he noticed, with a pang, how pretty she really was) stared at him disbelievingly; then, giving an odd, uneasy half smile, mumbled something about hoping she'd not given offence and wandered off to try her luck elsewhere.

She walked badly, as if she was coming to pieces, or, more likely, drunk. There was something familiar about her. Martin was certain he'd seen her before. Suddenly he remembered. She was the girl who usually sat with the threadbare old man and treated him to a night out.

She was parading the path that went round the mulberry tree, and presently she disappeared from view. He leaned forward, anxious to see if she reappeared round the other side.

An acquaintance walked by and smiled at him; Orpheus Jones let out a sour note, and the party of strangers at his usual place laughed over some private joke . . . Then she came back. He caught sight of her grey and yellow muslin gown, her wilting hat and the uncertain face beneath it, painted to represent pleasure.

She was still alone. Martin wondered if perhaps it was her first time? He saw her stop and try to pick up another man. She was trying that ugly devil who always sat by himself and never spoke to another living soul. It must be her first time, else she'd have known she'd have no luck there.

True enough. A look of fear and disgust came over the man's face, making it even uglier. He got up and almost ran away, as if the girl's smile might have infected him with the pox. She stood, staring after him with the same half smile that she'd given Martin. He saw her lips move and guessed that she was 'hoping she'd given no offence'.

'Come over here, lass!'

She whirled round in an absolute panic. For a moment she caught Martin's eye, and it was perfectly plain that she wondered if the summons had come from him.

'Over here! Over here, girl!'

The call had come from the party of strangers. She hesitated for an instant, and then went over to them. The party consisted of two women and three men, one of whom was little more than a youth. The girl waited, smiling uneasily while the party continued their conversation as if she wasn't there.

'Nice music, eh, Willie?' said one of the women to the youth, who was expensively but awkwardly dressed, as if his clothes were too stiff for him. He grinned happily and nodded, perhaps more vigorously than necessary.

The girl made as if to move away, but was bidden to wait.

'Feeling all right, lad?' inquired the older of the two men, leaning over and patting the youth on the arm. Again he grinned and gave his curiously vehement nod.

'Well, then, what about it?'

The man jerked his thumb towards the waiting girl; the two women giggled and blushed.

'What about it, Willie?' went on the man, with the utmost kindness. 'How would you like a real treat? Do you no end of good! It's high time you learned what it's for!'

They all laughed good-naturedly; then one of the women learned forward.

'I suppose she' (she indicated the girl with a movement of her head) 'she's *all right*?'

The man nodded. 'Quite right to ask.' He tipped back in his chair and addressed the girl for the first time since he'd called her over.

33

'No offence, lass, but are you *all right*? Clean, I mean. He's a bit simple, you see.' (He gestured to the grinning, nodding youth.) 'But he's as gentle as a lamb. No vice in him at all. He'll not have you up to any queer larks. And we won't argue about the money.'

'I suppose we're doing the right thing,' said the second woman doubtfully. 'But there can't be any harm in it. It's natural, after all. And it would be nice in the garden. Now, Willie dear – say good evening to the pretty lady.'

'G-g-good evening!' said the idiot; and grinned and nodded and laughed with all the good nature in the world.

Martin sat, frozen with shame and horror. He wanted to rush over and overturn the table and drive the vile strangers from the garden for ever. He wanted to seize the girl by the hand and drag her away to some bright, high place. But before he could so much as rise from his seat, the girl herself rendered his action superfluous.

She held up her hand, almost as if she was warding off a blow, then stumbled off as fast as she could. He caught a glimpse of her face. The lamp-black had started to run; she looked as though someone had half torn her eyes out.

The strangers appeared genuinely surprised; then irritation and finally concern for the rejected youth supervened. They went to endless trouble to comfort him and managed, at last, to satisfy him with a monstrous helping of cheesecake. Martin looked on and felt that he would never be able to eat it again as long as he lived.

He couldn't get the girl out of his mind. Her bewildered face and grey and yellow muslin dress haunted him. He wanted to get up and search for her. If only he'd spoken to her, even bought her that drink, then she'd have been spared the frightful humiliation she'd suffered.

He kept listening to the sounds that drifted from the

part of the garden to which she'd fled. He could hear the shrill laughter of apprentices and their lasses as they played at love-in-the-bushes. He didn't know what it was he hoped or feared to hear; the girl's voice had been too soft to have carried more than a few yards. All he knew was that he was obscurely frightened.

Suddenly he was sure he'd heard, amid all the shrill laughter, a scream of fright and pain. She'd been attacked! He stood up, spilling his glass of wine over his pale grey breeches. He looked round. No one else seemed to have heard anything. Laughing, smiling faces, eager with their own concerns everywhere. Could he perhaps have imagined it?

'Be quiet!' he wanted to cry out, when a waiter came officiously with water and a napkin to wipe away the wine stain.

'Did you – did you hear anything?'

'Hear what, Your Reverence?'

'That – ah! There it is again!'

It seemed to come from the booths. It was no longer a scream, but a shrill, breathy cry. It sounded like: 'Ife! Ife!'

Several people looked round, puzzled. Impatiently Martin pushed the waiter aside and began to walk rapidly towards the booths. He was shaking with anxiety.

'Ife! Ife!'

The cry was louder now. It was really impossible to say whether it was a man's or a woman's voice; there was so much air in it.

Martin hesitated. The sound was no longer from the booths but from behind the arbours. Now it seemed to be 'Life!' or 'Knife!'

It shifted again; it was circling the rotunda and drawing nearer and nearer. Orpheus Jones's voice faltered and the

35

music dwindled away. Then could be heard the unmistakable clatter of unsteady feet.

A moment later the general uneasiness gave way to comedy as into the lantern light came flying and flapping a youth with bright fair hair. He was dressed in only shirt and breeches and not very securely at that. He was as drunk as a lord, and pursued by all the terrors that dwell in the vine.

'Ife!' he hiccupped, and continued his wild progress round the mulberry tree.

'Disgusting!' said someone loudly, as the youth began to crash heedlessly into tables and chairs; and Martin sat down with a huge sigh of relief.

Only the idiot still showed signs of alarm at the wild gyrations of the drunkard, and resisted all the well-meaning attempts to make him laugh. He sat with wide-opened eyes as the youth, his hands clutching his shirt, began to splutter and choke. The drunkard's face had turned sweaty and was going that greenish yellow that betokens imminent sickness. Everyone who was near tried nervously to move out of range.

Two burly waiters, with expressions of haughty distaste and napkins at the ready, began to move towards the youth purposefully. He seemed to see them, for he made an enormous effort to control himself and actually tottered to something like a halt. His expression was unutterably dismayed.

'Ife!' he grunted, and collapsed a few yards from Martin Young. He lay quite still, face upwards and clutching at his shirt. Mercifully he had passed out before he'd had a chance to be sick.

'Now he'll sleep till Kingdom come!' said someone; and everyone relaxed into that good humoured toleration that the world extends to the sleeping drunkard.

The two waiters, having reached their objective, exchanged resigned glances and bent down to carry it away.

'My God!' muttered one of them. 'Look at this, mate!'

A small handle had been sticking up between the youth's fingers; as the waiter pulled it away, a great flower of blood blossomed out all over his shirt. The youth's eyes flickered; then they ceased to shine.

'It's all right, Willie! It's nothing, lad! It's only wine! It's all a game! Laugh, Willie! For God's sake, laugh!'

One of the waiters, whiter than his napkin, approached Martin.

'Your Reverence . . . can you come, sir? You being a magistrate . . . That young man, sir. He's dead. He's been stabbed . . . murdered!'

Martin stood up, acutely conscious of the wine stain on his breeches.

'Certainly . . . certainly.'

Those who had crowded round the body made way respectfully for the youthful priest-magistrate. They smiled at him, a little timidly; his presence at such a time was both reassuring and solemn.

The waiter, who had removed the knife and was actually still holding it, moved back and joined his fellow as Martin knelt down beside the dead youth.

He looked unreal, doll-like . . . so that even his spreading blood in the lantern-light looked like wine. Martin knew he should be feeling pity and anger in the face of such a crime; but he could only feel a dull and confused relief that he was confronted with the body of a stranger.

He looked away from the intolerable stupidity of the dead face to the hands which somehow still seemed to have intelligence and gesturing eloquence. They were still fixed in the attitude of clutching the knife they had failed to halt. But there was something else between the fingers. A fragment of cloth; a small, torn piece of grey and yellow muslin. It was from a woman's dress.

He saw, with extraordinary clarity, the look of shame and humiliation on the face of the girl who'd fled from the idiot; and he heard again the distant scream of terror. He knew, beyond all possible doubt, that she, and she alone, had committed this crime in the panic of her flight. The youth had accosted her; perhaps tried to drag her clothing off ... and she had done this to defend herself. He knew also that he himself had been partly to blame; though his guilt in the affair was only answerable to heaven.

He heard voices murmuring above him as he knelt; he could hear the waiters being officious, and someone asking to be let through.

He touched one of the dead hands and found it to be, shockingly, lukewarm. He pulled at the fingers, which opened out as easily as the petals of a flower. He noted that the first and second fingers of the right hand were deeply scored, as if in the exercise of some trade.

'Look, look,' he murmured, half to himself. 'Do you see this?' – as if to impress everyone near that there were no secrets he was unwilling to share.

At the same time his other hand rested on the youth's left hand, covering it as if to afford comfort. His fingers encountered the piece of muslin. Gently, and almost without realizing what he was doing, he pulled it free and crumpled it up inside his fist.

He stood up and thrust his fist into his breeches pocket. Although he was certain that no one could have seen this action, he felt a sudden chill sweep across him. He remembered this sensation in great detail afterwards; it was exactly as he imagined it might have been if grace had been suddenly withdrawn from him. But another and perhaps more reasonable explanation was that, in that moment, he understood the enormity of what he had done, and, like Cain of old, could not escape the feeling that there *had* been a witness.

'This is Dr Dormann, Your Reverence,' said one of the garden's servants. 'Dr Dormann is in charge here . . .'

A man, thin as a bone and in black, came towards him. A hand, like a white spider, was outstretched. Martin made an effort to withdraw his clenched fist from his pocket; but the bloodstained fragment of muslin had stuck to his palm. Dr Dormann lowered his hand.

'There is blood on your . . . breeches, Mr Young,' he said with quiet concern, as if it was the most important thing in the world.

Martin looked down; he was panic-stricken that the evidence he'd hidden had leaked through and was betraying itself.

'No, no! It's wine. It's red wine I spilled earlier! For God's sake, stop that boy laughing! Stop him, I say!'

The idiot had succumbed at last to the kindly persuasion of his companions and abandoned himself to a fierce merriment. Apologetically his companions began to lead him away.

'The garden must be searched,' said Martin, the idiot's voice dinning in his head. 'There might still be evidence . . .'

'Yes . . . there might be evidence,' repeated Dr Dormann; and for a moment the man possessed by a devil and the man possessed by an angel stared into each other's eyes, while peal after peal of the idiot's laughter echoed in the colonnades and down the winding walks.

Chapter Four

MRS BRAY was shaken, dismayed; she was like a huge
tree across which a storm had passed, leaving it broken-
branched and weeping leaves in the sullen aftermath.

Refusing to emerge, she sat in her upstairs parlour while
her garden was scoured by order of the law. She kept
staring into a tortoiseshell looking-glass, which she clutched
in her hand as if it was a talisman and begged, of her own
reflection, it seemed, that her dead husband and her live
children might not be dragged out into the countless pry-
ing lights. Then she put the glass away and sat by the
window, reduced to nothing more than a dark, gigantic
shudder.

Her prayers were answered. Nothing was discovered;
Mr Bray still slept and the skilful children remained unseen. She calmed down and began to breathe more easily,

exuding sandalwood perfume like a huge midnight flower. When Dr Dormann came to tell her that the worst was over and that everyone had gone, he thought she'd dozed off. Gently he intimated that the children had been summoned.

'Not tonight, Dr D. Not after that horrible thing.'

'But what if one of them –?'

'– I know what you're thinking, Dr D. It's downright wicked. It would be blood-money. I'd sooner not, Dr D. You know how I like to keep what's not right from the children. But on the other hand, I don't see how it can be helped. Not now, that is . . .'

The scene in the cellar was subdued. The children sat on their benches uneasily. They were really frightened, not by what had happened, but by the troubled air of Mrs Bray herself. Not even the ritual drinking of the mulberry cordial served to enliven them beyond an occasional squabble. The only circumstance that remained unchanged was the lateness of Briskitt. This time it passed all bounds and he missed his drink.

At length he came clattering down the steps and appeared, bursting with excuses and apologies. It seemed that, in order to elude the scouring of the garden, he'd got himself embroiled in a remote bush so deeply that he'd had real fears of being growed all over and greened to death.

'But better late than never,' he ended up, after demonstrating the various wounds he had sustained in the service of the garden.

Dr Dormann dismissed him and he took his place with an enormous wink at his colleagues.

Mrs Bray sighed. 'Now we are all here,' she began, gently pushing away the ledger that Dr Dormann had placed before her, 'there is something I must say to you.' She sighed again; it was plain that she really was reluctant

41

to broach the subject. 'There has been something very disagreeable happen in our garden. A wicked, dirty thing.'

She paused and rubbed her eyes with a perfect gargoyle of a fist. In her own extraordinary way, she had a very real regard for her children's tender years. Although they witnessed, nightly, more casual sins than many a grown man might see in a lifetime, Mrs Bray honestly felt they were preserved from corruption by the air of the Mulberry Garden itself. It was all a game . . .

'Who killed Cock Robin?' she asked playfully. 'Who saw him die?'

No one answered. Dr Dormann turned the pages of the ledger.

'Come, now,' urged Mrs Bray, clasping her hands together. 'Is there none of you to answer? Ain't no one going to say: "I said the fly, with my little eye"? Ain't there a little fly in my garden?' She paused and fluttered her clasped fingers encouragingly. 'Little fly? Little fly?'

The children stared at her fingers, but made no answer.

'All right,' said Mrs Bray at length. 'But please to remember that if there is a little fly, and he's not telling, he ought to bear in mind that there's someone who's watching him all the time. There's no secrets from Mr Bray. *He* can see you wherever you are!'

She turned to Dr Dormann who pushed the ledger before her again. She glanced down and then looked back at her assistant.

'Why have you done that?' she asked angrily.

'What, ma'am?'

'You know! Opened it at *that page*!'

'I'm sorry – I'm sorry. I didn't mean to . . .'

The garden was quiet and airless, as though a hole had been torn in its fabric and all its breath had leaked away.

The colonnades glimmered feebly in the starlight and the booths had a forlorn, bankrupt air. Only the chairs, the tumbled, forgotten chairs, still seemed aghast at the scene they had witnessed.

Dr Dormann passed them by. The arbours yawned for him, ineffably mysterious, inviting, engulfing . . . He trembled and quickened his pace until he reached the rotunda; and then it was as if he had been caught in a wind that blew him round and round like a long, black leaf. At last his gyrations – which were like a light-footed parody of the motions of the murdered youth – ceased. He knelt down beside a chalked cross; it was the place where the youth had fallen and had been marked for the benefit of the coroner.

Dr Dormann shut his eyes and laced his fingers together in an attitude of prayer. So tightly was he pressing that it was a marvel that his knuckle bones didn't jump through his skin. He was attempting to reconstruct the scene of the tragedy.

Little by little, as he worked at it, the scene began to build itself in his memory; groups, objects and finally actions returning, at first fleetingly and then with some degree of clarity and permanence. To each of these group-ings he bestowed a final, inner, glance, almost as if to fix them before sharpening his mind to cut more deeply.

Now he saw the figure of the priest-magistrate bending down beside the body. He saw his hands move . . .

'That's it! That's it!' he whispered triumphantly; and Martin Young obligingly went through his part in the scene again. 'Now stop there!' And Martin stopped, right hand outstretched.

Cautiously and justly the thinker examined the scene in meticulous detail, as if aware that the slightest unclear thought would disperse it for ever.

43

'Again! Again!' he breathed; and Martin Young began to jerk back and forth inside his head. Now he was touching the dead hand; now he was not. Touch – let go! Touch – let go!

A fluttering had begun to appear, a fragile wisp of something that at one moment was attached to one hand and then to the other. At first it was like a strand of smoke or an emanation; then it became coloured, yellow and grey. It was a piece of torn paper . . . no! It was a fragment of cloth!

He had snatched it from the dead hand. Why? He had recognized it. He had been frightened by it; so he had taken it and hidden it. He had committed the beginning of a crime. The man possessed by a devil exulted as the man possessed by an angel was caught inside his head.

'It's no good to either man or beast, Dr D.'

Dr Dormann shuddered violently and opened his eyes as he heard Mrs Bray's voice. The scene in his mind fled into tatters. He stood up. His mistress was in the rotunda. For all he knew she had been there all the time. He dreaded she'd witnessed his thoughts.

'They'll go poking around again tomorrow, I expect,' she said plaintively.

'It will soon be over, ma'am.'

'People will stay away. Nobody likes a murder. And what with the law turning us inside out . . . What if they close us down?'

'You mustn't think of that!'

'How can I help it when they've gone and poked him – it – that horrible thing down underneath in the chair store?' She gestured to the room below the rotunda where the corpse had been stowed until the morning.

'It's a warm night and I'm sure I can smell it. A smell

44

like that don't go away. It clings to everything. What if our people smell it tomorrow?'

She lapsed into silence and then began again: 'And another thing. I didn't like the reverend being mixed up in it. I told you about my dream; that blood on his page in the ledger. What does it all mean? I'm frightened half to death, Dr D.'

'There's no need . . . no need, ma'am.'

'Don't you talk to me about need! You just do as you're told and keep your nose clean, my friend! And don't you go monkeying with that page again!'

Dr Dormann looked up to his immense mistress with something like anguish. Grotesque as she was, he all but worshipped her. She alone in his dark world held out the offer of peace and warmth. Did he want to become her lover? The thought fascinated and terrified him. All he knew was that he wanted to serve her to the last drop of his strength. He dared not tell her how close he was to ruining her enemy; she would be so angry with him if he failed. She would cast him out, and that would be the end . . .

'Fireworks,' said the rotunda, broodily.

'What, ma'am?' Mrs Bray's changes of subject were sometimes confusing in their abruptness.

'I said fireworks, Dr D. I've been thinking it over. We'll have a show of fireworks. Mr Bray always said there's nothing like fireworks to clear the air, and get rid of nasty smells. And it takes people's minds off things. Mr Cuper does fireworks very reasonable. You go and see what twenty pounds will buy, Dr D. Rockets and serpents and them things that go round and round. But no bangs, mind! We mustn't frighten the children . . .'

She never forgot the children or their welfare. She regarded herself as their earth, or garden, mother; and, as

45

such, she took precedence over any lesser mothers they might privately have. This was Mrs Bray's solemn belief; and it was the children's, too. One and all, they would have swum the wide Thames at Mrs Bray's bidding, while for the mothers who'd actually borne them, they wouldn't even have crossed a rainy street.

Yet in spite of this, there was no doubt that the ownership of a private mother was, among the children, regarded as something of a distinction; obscurely they felt it lent them a certain cachet.

Now Briskitt, being one of those not so distinguished, definitely felt at a social disadvantage; consequently he had been shrewd enough to select, as the friend of his bosom, an infant with an undoubted ma in Bridewell Gaol.

It was Briskitt's well-thought-out plan to indulge this infant – who was known as Chops on account of his association with Briskitt – with little delicacies to take into the gaol for his ma. Regularly he spent most of his nightly sixpences on such treats, it being in Briskitt's mind that, by placing Chop's ma under an obligation, he was securing her by a process of hire purchase.

He had actually seen Chops's ma, so there was no question of a pig in a poke. He'd seen her and been deeply impressed. She'd been the third one down in a line of hemp-beaters: a sweet, mulberry-cheeked dolly with tits like pillows and eyes like pots of jam.

Chops, on the other hand, for whom usage had dulled appreciation, could see nothing in his ma worth more than a fart. So he was deeply flattered by Briskitt's attention, as Briskitt was the senior imp of the garden and an object of veneration to his fellows on account of his habitual lateness and unfailing impertinence to Dr Dormann. Everyone thought that Briskitt could have shamed the devil; but not in any derogatory sense, of course.

'Was you really stuck in a bush?' asked Chops, paying his nightly call on his patron in the stables before returning to the bosom of his ma in gaol.

'Walls 'ave ears,' said Briskitt, crouching in his nest of straw like a peculiarly venomous horse-fly.

'Then you wasn't!' deduced Chops with awe.

''Ow's our ma?' asked Briskitt, changing the subject dexterously.

'All right, I s'pose.'

'Then give 'er this!' said Briskitt magnificently. 'An' tell 'er it's from 'er lovin' Briskitt.'

He pushed something into Chops's ever-willing hand.

'Cor!' breathed Chops. 'It's a pound, ain't it?'

'It's what you calls a guinea,' corrected Briskitt. 'An' 'ere's another. Tell 'er to buy 'erself somethin' pretty.'

'Cor!' repeated Chops, dividing his amazement between his patron and the two gold coins in his filthy palm. 'Did you nick 'em, Briskitt?'

'I don't give our ma things what's nicked,' said Briskitt with dignity. 'You tell 'er Briskitt earned it.'

'How? Go on! Tell us how?'

Briskitt smiled kindly. He was moved by Chops's admiration, but at the same time he would not betray a confidence.

'Piss off!' he said affably. 'You jus' go back an' tell our ma there's more where that came from! Tell 'er that – that Briskitt's made 'is pile!'

So Chops, knowing that further entreaty would be in vain, departed for the gaol, leaving his patron in a state of deep and ecstatic thought.

Briskitt had a secret; not only from Chops, but from the world as well. He had found the goose that laid golden eggs.

Straying – as he often did – from the twelfth arbour, he

had chanced to witness something so extraordinary that it fair took his breath away. He had seen the murder!

For a moment he'd just stood and gaped. He couldn't believe it had happened. 'Cor!' he'd said, before he could stop himself.

'Who's that? Who's there?'

'Cor!'

'It's a child! Oh my God! It's a child!'

'Wodjer done? Wodjer done?'

'Please – please don't give me away! Please! Please!'

'Cor! You're cryin'!'

'Look! Look! Here's money! It's all I've got! Take it! I'll bring you more! I swear it!'

'When?' asked Briskitt, undeniably influenced.

'Next Friday! Every Friday! I'll bring you money every Friday!'

'Cor! Promise?'

'Yes – yes! And you? Will you promise? You won't breathe a word?'

'Fridy to Fridy. So longs as you keeps comin'. I promise.'

'God bless you for that!'

'Cor!'

So Briskitt, in exchange for his solemn word, had made his pile. Now, as he lay in the straw, clutching a further two gold coins he'd prudently withheld from Chops, dreams of an intensely romantic nature filled his heart. He dreamed of riding a white horse straight into Bridewell Gaol, up the steps and into the Governor's parlour, and there purchasing the freedom of 'our ma'.

Chapter Five

THE management of Martin Young's household was in the hand, under God, of Mrs Jackson. He had kept a long-standing promise to her that, one day, when he was grown up, she should come back and keep house for him. She was the Scottish nurse whom he had never forgotten since their tearful farewells on the occasion of her dismissal. Martin, who possessed the warmest of natures, had been really attached to her, and one of the chief pleasures of his independence had been to offer his old nurse employment as his housekeeper. Mrs Jackson, receiving his letter, abandoned the family she was serving and rushed upon Clerkenwell as if by Divine command.

'I always knew it! I always knew it!' she sobbed. 'That we'd be together here or in heaven!'

To her, Martin the grown man was the worthy child to the ethereal little father she had nursed so long ago. She revelled in the respect that was accorded to him . . . and turned no charitable object from the vicarage door who might conceivably have redounded to her master's credit in heaven. She gave of his substance without stint. It was like the loaves and fishes all over again; and she was the privileged dispenser.

Smilingly he put up with it, and went about his parish duties confident in the knowledge that there would be company when he got home.

The aged, the infirm, the troubled, the frightened and the lost were always waiting for him in a small, bare room with whitewashed walls that adjoined the kitchen. Although little enough was required of him (Mrs Jackson was concerned not to overtire her master and would have fed the visitors), it was still an effort of will to look in and smile and say something sensible and, if possible, helpful. On these occasions Mrs Jackson would stand behind him, like a stage manager watching an inspired performer whose talent never ceased to surprise and delight. And somehow it never failed. Whatever of fretfulness or distress had been in the room vanished, and a sense of peace and comfort took its place.

'There, now!' she'd murmur, her face shining like a well-polished pippin. 'There, now!'

In addition to this, the good old woman's pride and superstitiously devout nature led her to boast about her master to the servants; and several times Martin had overheard, to his mild indignation, certain events of his own childhood earnestly recounted as if they'd come straight from a Calendar of Saints.

In short, she troubled him, embarrassed him and sometimes maddened him; but he would never have dreamed of letting her see it. He respected her and even loved her for her simplicity and the steadfast faith she had in his God-given talent.

On the night of the murder in the garden, he returned to the vicarage much beyond his usual hour.

'There was two puir bodies waiting,' said Mrs Jackson, with a hint of reproach. 'But I had to send 'em away, master.'

She would never call him Mr Martin, but insisted, with an obstinate smile, on 'master'.

Martin nodded gratefully and explained the tragic reason for his lateness while she bustled to and fro to set his meal before him. She listened with half an ear, shaking her head from time to time in distress. It was not the crime that upset her, but her master's being involved in it. She had never entirely resigned herself to Martin's becoming a magistrate; she had a deep mistrust of the law which, to her, lacked gentleness and sometimes took the name of the Lord in vain.

'I can see it's sapped you, master,' she said when Martin had finished his account, omitting, of course, his own extraordinary action in concealing material evidence. 'Your eyes looked tired . . . like St Peter after he'd wrastled wi' the de'il.'

'Surely you mean Jacob?' said Martin wearily.

'Jacob wrastled wi' the angel, master. I was talking of St Peter of Hoy who wrastled wi' the de'il up in Scourie and tossed him into the sea. They say he came back wi' eyes like moons and his breeches stained wi' bluid from the de'il's heel . . .'

'But it's only wine, Mrs Jackson. I spilled a glass of wine.'

She nodded; but Martin felt that nothing he could say would convince her that he had not undergone a supernatural experience, similar to that enjoyed by St Peter of Hoy.

He went upstairs and began to undress mechanically, when Mrs Jackson knocked on his door.

'If ye'll leave out them breeches, master, I'll see if the stain canna be washed away.'

He emptied the pocket, and withdrew the blood-stained fragment of muslin. He stared down at it, bewildered anew by what he had done. He remembered, with unpleasant clarity, the sudden, sweeping chill he'd felt as he'd taken the tell-tale piece of the girl's dress from the dead hand. Could it be possible that he had, in that inexplicable moment, really endangered or even lost something that was infinitely valuable? Had his old nurse, in some uncanny way, divided this?

But he had not done anything wrong. He had been perfectly within his rights, as the representative of the law, to take charge of a piece of evidence.

(Why had that man in black stared at him so intently, and stressed the word: 'evidence'?)

All he need do was to find the girl and exert such spiritual powers as he possessed to bring her to confess her crime. If she came forward, at once and of her own free will, she might very well escape the extreme penalty of the law.

(How horrible if she were to be hanged! He tried to shut out the vision of her pretty face, bloated and purple, her eyes glaring and her pleasant body writhing and dancing in furious ignomy.)

But this was a chimera! There was every reason for her to be saved. He himself would give evidence on her behalf. He would explain the humiliations she'd suffered and support her plea of self-defence. He had only taken the piece of muslin to prevent a miscarriage of justice.

(Yet he might have left it there for all to see. There was no need for him to have acted like a thief.)

He had done nothing wrong; that was the important thing. If he had, in some way unknown to him, wrestled with the devil, then he had won. The wine stain on his breeches had been symbolic; it had been the devil, and not the Lamb of God who'd bled. He would find the girl to-morrow . . .

He put the piece of muslin carefully behind a mirror; later, when it was safe and he had more time, he would find a better hiding-place.

In the morning, before the eleven o'clock service, he visited the coroner and laid before him all the information he considered necessary. The coroner thanked him and, after consulting his diary, suggested that the inquest might be held on the Tuesday to come. He hoped that would give Mr Young sufficient time to pursue any inquiries he considered relevant?

'Oh yes, yes!'

'You have some suspicions, then?'

'I – I am not sure.'

The coroner nodded. Had the weather been cooler, he might have been able to stretch a point for another couple of days; but . . . He spread out his hands and then delicately held his nose. Martin agreed that it had better be Tuesday. He stood up and shook hands with the coroner.

'It's an extraordinary thing . . . your coming to see me, Mr Young. I was intending to visit you this morning.'

'Why? Whatever for?'

'My wife. She is passing through a difficult time, you understand. At the moment it's very bad. She would like to see you. She always says that there's something about you that calms her and helps her through the worst. It's a great gift you have, Mr Young!'

'Of course I'll see her!' said Martin eagerly.

'She's upstairs, in bed. We'd both be grateful for your time.'

Martin hastened up to see the woman possessed by intangible fears and miseries. Her curtains were drawn so that the room was in darkness; she had a headache that felt as if there was a maggot in her brain.

'Is that you, Mr Young?'

'Yes. May I sit by you?'

'Please . . . please. I feel so terrible . . . so miserable and empty of everything. And I'm in such pain. I want to die . . . I want to be finished with everything. What use is my life? I make everyone unhappy about me . . .'

'Is the pain very bad?'

'Yes.'

'Would you like me to read to you?'

'The service for the sick?'

'No. I wasn't thinking of that.'

'What then?'

'A pleasant story. Something with a happy ending . . .'

'I'm not a child.'

'No?'

'I am old enough to be your mother . . .'

'I wish you were; my mother, I mean.'

'Why do you say that?'

'I don't know. It was just the way you looked at me. I'm sorry; I'm not being very helpful, am I?'

'More than you think. Will you put your hand on my forehead . . . just for a moment. Then I'll let you go.'

'I'm not a healer, you know.'

'You are better than that. You help us to heal ourselves.'

Martin left the coroner's house at a quarter to eleven. He felt that to have been called upon to exercise his gift at such a time was an omen and a promise. He had almost three days in which to find the girl before the inquest made it necessary for him to give up the evidence against her.

At first he thought he might return to the Mulberry Garden and question the waiters who surely knew her. But then, he reflected, such a course would draw attention to his own suspicions and endanger the girl needlessly. There was no need for that. His duties in the parish took him far and wide; he was confident he would find her, if not today, then tomorrow . . .

His talent remained with him undiminished; it was not so fragile a thing as he had feared. He returned to the church and, after the service, hid the bloodstained fragment of muslin in the vestry among his surplices. He felt that he was offering it as a hostage, until the Tuesday . . .

Chapter Six

THE ripples created by the murder spread far beyond the confines of Clerkenwell. The nature of the crime – the splash of blood in the midst of the innocent gaiety of a pleasure garden – was such as to provoke interest and conjecture among a wide variety of people. It was, or it became, everyman's crime. It had something for the puritan and something for the sybarite; it was a young man's crime; it was an old man's crime; and it was, of course, a woman's crime. In short, it was a love crime . . . and all the world loves a lover. A journalist wrote a short poem on it, and it was mentioned in at least one sermon – though not by Martin Young. Philosophers found in it a comment on the state of society, and everyone else a reminder of the dark dangers of sex.

The murdered youth turned out to have been a staymaker's apprentice from Goswell Street by the name of

Isaac Fisk. He had been seventeen years old and as insignificant as any of the thousands of apprentices who made nuisances of themselves in the steets of the town. But now, in the space of two or three days, he had become as well known as the Archbishop of Canterbury. The brutal murder of a couple in the Haymarket (for the gain of five shillings) passed unremarked, and all the town, in spirit if not in body, attended the inquest on the youth who had been slain in the Mulberry Garden.

Among the witnesses summoned to attend the inquest, which was to be held in the upstairs room of the Red Rose in Bridewell Alley, was one Major Smith, who had given his address as care of A. Woodcock, of Ludgate Hill, and thereafter sweated with fear. When the court's messenger called, on the Monday morning, the woollen draper panicked. He was convinced that the very mention of Major Smith shrieked his sinful duplicity from the housetops; he couldn't believe that his apprentice, who appeared from behind a roll of cloth, had not overheard the whole transaction and now read the guilt in his eyes.

But that industrious youth, who always nursed a dread that anything of a mysterious nature must be working for his downfall, jumped to the conclusion that the paper his master had thrust fiercely into his pocket was something to do with him; and when, on the following morning, Mr Woodcock put on a coat of military cut and prepared to go out, he worried himself sick that his master was off to interview a possible replacement. Consequently he redoubled his efforts to become indispensable and 'make a go of things'.

'And would it be c'rect, sir, to knock a shillin' a yard horf the green worsted if the horder is in hexcess of ten pund? And should I hextend the 'ouse's credit to military gentlemen hover the rank of capting? And I won't stir for

56

me dinner, sir, unless the young ladies is hagreeable to mindin' the shop. Or would you sooner I locked up and lef' a notice to hexplain? I'd be hobliged for your advice, sir . . .'

The woollen draper glared at the youth whose mean soul seemed to possess no spark of imagination or human feeling.

'Stay in the shop,' he snarled. 'You can wait for your dinner till I get back.'

Bridewell Alley, a narrow grin of a passage between the prison and the Quaker workhouse, was crowded with eyes, all of which fixed themselves on Major Smith as he entered the Red Rose and crept up the stairs. As he entered the steamy, crowded room, every face turned to stare at him with accusation and contempt. He quailed and sank into obscurity somewhere at the back.

The proceedings opened with formal evidence of identity, given by the youth's employer. Then came the calling of witnesses and the last moments of Isaac Fisk were laboriously pieced together: the first glimpse of him staggering out into the lantern light, his wild dance and his final collapse and death.

Major Smith, having had no choice but to swear to a false name, gave his evidence badly. He couldn't rid himself of the horrible sensation that 'A. Woodcock, draper; wife and three daughters', was written all over him in letters of fire. He kept feeling that, any moment, the coroner was going to lean forward and ask him searchingly if he was sure his name was Major Smith? 'This is madness, madness!' a voice hissed inside his head; and, when at last he was allowed to go back to his place, he swore to God that, if he escaped the dangers of this day, he would never go back to the Mulberry Garden again.

He slumped down in his seat; then, after a little while, he sat upright and began to look round to see if Leila Robinson had come. He thought he saw her, but he couldn't be sure: all women look alike during the day . . .

After the Major came Tom Hastey and his Lucy, who could offer so little that they would seem to be wasting the court's time. Yet the coroner treated them with indulgence.

Of all the Friday-nighters, they suffered least from being drawn into the light of day. They were the young lovers, the spirit of the garden against which the offence had been committed. Obscurely everyone felt that their presence was important; it made the crime seem worse, as if it was an insult offered to the harmless and beautiful.

The garden itself treasured them. Although their secret intimacies were well known to Mrs Bray, she would never have sent Dr Dormann to call upon them. They were inviolate, there was not even a page for them in the ledger.

Of course it was well known that their love was a hopeless case. Tom Hastey, by the world's standards, was a fool and would never amount to more than the coal-merchant's clerk that he was; and Lucy was little more than a flower-faced simpleton bewitched by the charm of youth. But this very hopelessness made their love seem all the more precious.

'It's not for us to put more pricks in their bed of roses,' Mrs Bray used to declare. 'Leave the darlings be!'

Now the waiters were called, and those who had helped to search the garden. At this point the room became intent, for something odd had mysteriously emerged. Where was Isaac Fisk's coat? No trace of it had been found. The gate-keeper, a most conscientious man, swore that no one had entered the garden without wearing a coat. It was not

58

allowed. Yet the dead youth had been dressed only in his shirt and breeches.

Was it possible, perhaps, that the deceased had entered the garden without passing the gate-keeper? There was only one entrance to the garden; it was otherwise encircled by a high wall, rimmed with broken glass. Could not the deceased, being young and agile, have climbed the wall and used his coat to muffle the glass? the coroner suggested. Certainly it was possible; but even so, what had become of the coat? It had vanished, it seemed, off the face of the earth.

Two friends of the deceased, nervous and embarrassed, gave evidence that it had always been the custom for the three of them to meet in the garden on Friday nights. But on this night he'd failed to meet them, even though he'd promised to come. The first they'd known of his presence was when they'd seen him, lying dead under the mulberry tree. They couldn't understand it . . .

As they talked about him, with evident affection, a new ghost seemed to enter the room . . . an extension backwards in time of the tottering, nameless, dying object seen and described by all. This new ghost was that of a deftly dancing young man, a jesting, carefree young man, a young man without an enemy in the world.

Yet here was the knife (examined and sworn to by a surgeon and thereafter passed among the jury) that had entered this youth without an enemy in the world below the left nipple to a depth of three and a quarter inches and a width of a quarter of an inch.

It was, as the jury saw, a common, bone-handled knife such as might have been used for cutting fruit or sharpening pens. It was worth no more than sixpence, the blade having been ground down so often that it was scarcely broader than a bodkin.

With such an unusually sharp weapon no great strength

59

would have been required to inflict the blow. The blade had scarcely touched the fourth rib and must have gone in very easily indeed. In all probability the deceased himself would not have realized that he'd been murdered until that terrible moment when the soul leaves the body.

This expression, carrying with it so solemn an implication, produced a silence in the room, so that the witness who followed the surgeon was greeted with an awe that was touched with eternity.

'Do you swear that the evidence which you shall give this inquest, on behalf of our Sovereign Lord the King, touching the death of Isaac Fisk, shall be the truth, the whole truth, and nothing but the truth: so help you God?'

'I do,' said Martin Young, staring at the door and the faces in the room with an anguish he could not quite conceal.

He had not found her. He had scoured the parish; he had neglected his duties; he had waited outside the garden each night, praying for the girl to appear. Even now, he hoped that, by some miracle, she would walk through the door and give herself up.

He had not brought the piece of cloth with him; in the agitation of the morning he had forgotten it. But that didn't matter. He would explain that he'd forgotten it and would bring it to the coroner's house. To forget was no crime.

He answered the coroner's questions in a voice that was scarcely audible; twice the foreman of the jury asked him to speak up. He gave the impression of one who was worn out and whose mind could only with difficulty be brought to bear on the matter in hand. He sensed that everyone's sympathy was with him and no one liked to see him exposed to ceaseless questions.

He dreaded the moment when the coroner should ask

him if there was anything else he thought might be relevant. He kept glancing pleadingly at the door. If only she would come!

His mouth felt terribly dry and he had to ask for a glass of water. The coroner sympathized; the room was very hot. Martin had the impression that the coroner was on the point of letting him go, when someone said:

'Might I be allowed to ask Mr Young a question?'

Martin shuddered, and the chill he had felt once before swept over him. The questioner was Dr Dormann. Although the man was not even looking at him – he was gazing inquiringly at the coroner – Martin felt a force of concentration and enmity directed against him such as he had never known before in his life.

'If your question has a bearing, sir.'

'It does indeed. I wanted to ask the witness if, when he examined the body, he noticed anything caught in the dead man's hands?'

'Why should you ask that?'

'It is just that I thought it possible that he might have caught hold of something – a piece of cloth, for example – from his murderer's, or murderess's, clothing. A fragment of material torn from a sleeve. Something of the kind might easily have been overlooked.'

'I cannot think it very likely, sir. But, nevertheless, I will put your question to Mr Young. Did you, Mr Young, notice anything of the kind?'

'I – I am trying to remember . . . There was a great deal of blood, you know . . . I – I –'

Please God let her come in now! Please God let her be saved! Don't let me have to send her out in the hangman's cart to be strangled till her life streams away!

'Could the witness speak up?' said the foreman of the jury.

'I saw nothing,' said Martin. 'There was . . . nothing in – in his hands.'

Involuntarily he raised his hand to his mouth as the perjury escaped him. But it was too late; and for a moment he had the feeling of something huge and black sweeping into the crowded room and gathering up his words. He saw Dr Dormann's face; it was dead white and triumphant. Martin flinched, fully expecting the man to stand up and accuse him of perjury . . .

But Dr Dormann said nothing. The extreme pallor of his face was accompanied by a freezing sensation within. He knew that one of his attacks was imminent . . .

'Fetch a glass of brandy!' he heard someone say.

'No . . . no. I am all right, now,' someone answered. 'It was the heat. I'll sit down . . .'

'But I am sitting down,' said Dr Dormann; and then understood that the second voice had not been his – as he'd supposed – but the witness's. It seemed that Martin Young had all but fainted.

Shortly before one o'clock, the jury brought in their verdict. They found that, on the night of 16 August, in the Mulberry Pleasure Garden, at about a quarter to eleven o'clock, a certain person unknown had struck Isaac Fisk below the left nipple to a depth of three and a quarter inches and a width of a quarter of an inch, with a common, bone-handled knife worth perhaps sixpence; and that from this wound, the said Isaac Fisk had languished and died. And that the said person unknown, after he or she had committed the said felony in the manner aforesaid, did flee away: against the peace of our Lord the King, his crown and dignity.

'Have you anything to add?' asked the coroner.

The foreman nodded. 'It is our opinion that, taking into

account the nature of the place where the crime was committed and that the deceased was partly undressed, it was a love crime. It is our opinion that the murder was committed by a woman who afterwards carried away the deceased's coat under her gown, most likely with the object of selling it.'

As the crowd surged out and down the stairs, a voice cried out: 'See you Friday, dear!' and Major Smith, the first perjurer, turned to see Leila Robinson's unmistakable hand waving to him from the top of the stairs. Eagerly he waved back, and at once absolved himself from the solemn promise he'd made before.

'It wasn't,' he said to himself over and over again as he returned to Ludgate Hill, 'as if I'd actually sworn on a Bible. And we're all only human, after all.'

Chapter Seven

'Are you quite well? –'

'Why not wait a while?'

'Can I help you home? My carriage –'

Martin shrank from the kindly offers of assistance. He moved back; he could not bear to be touched, even. He felt naked and ashamed. He left the place of the inquest alone and hurried along Bridewell Alley. By the time he had reached the corner, he found himself to be almost running.

At once there flashed upon his mind the madness of criminals who draw needless suspicion upon themselves by running – running, as if the hounds of hell were after them, when there was nothing to fear but the shadows within themselves.

He wondered how many other signs would mark him out? Would his eyes show that flickering fear of discovery he'd seen so often when he sat on the Bench?

He glanced helplessly behind him to see if Dr Dormann was following. A dozen loiterers outside the Red Rose stared after him. He attempted to dissemble with a smile, and they looked away.

He began to walk the streets and alleys and courts about Bridewell Gaol – places he knew like the back of his hand; but somehow it seemed a different hand. Familiar sights became strange in their very familiarity, like reflections in a crooked mirror. He found himself in dead ends – wrinkled passages that ended up as black as a boot. He came upon children, ancient little children, squatting on steps, pissing in corners, or just standing and staring with eyes like stone. He must have seen them many times before; he liked children, and they in turn liked him. But suddenly they were strangers and did not answer his strained smile.

He paused at the head of a flight of steps that led down to a gin cellar. Again it was a place he'd visited on several occasions to bring comfort to the dying. He was known there ... but not now. Three figures, two men and a woman, stood in the cellar doorway and stared up as if he wasn't there. He could see the woman was marked down for a painful and disgusting death. Her skin had the fatal yellowish tinge and she nursed her swollen liver as if it had been a child. He stretched out his hand, pleading to be of help. For an instant she caught his eye, shrugged her shoulders and smiled bitterly; then she turned and went back into the cellar.

He went on till he came to St John's Street and suddenly he thought he saw the girl he'd been seeking. It was her figure and her walk. He ran after her, drew level and looked in her face. It was savage with disease. She answered his look with a bony smile, and asked if he'd like to share what she'd caught off such as him? She was drunk, of course, and did not know what she was saying ...

He walked back, past the end of Bull Yard, a well-known market place for whores. A group of them, perhaps half a dozen, were congregated on the corner of the Yard, obstructing the entrance and spilling over the pavement. As Martin approached, they made no effort to move out of his way; they seemed dazed with the curious arrogance of their trade ... or perhaps, more likely, by the sweetish, faintly herbal smell of the nearby gin distillery.

He wanted to ask them to let him by, as the street in that part was fouled by dogs and horses. But he found himself frightened to speak to them. It was a feeling he couldn't explain ...

The women, seeing his hesitation, grinned at him and one of them hitched up her skirt, revealing a tantalizing glimpse of filthy petticoat and a torn black stocking through which her flesh appeared in shining islands.

'I – I –' he began; when she laughed and dropped her skirt.

'Make way for 'is lordship, girls! Don't go pushin' 'im in the shit!'

He walked by them with his head down and over-whelmed with shame. Afterwards he thought he should have asked them if they knew the girl he was looking for. But how would he have described her? He remembered her walk, her height and the colour of the dress she'd worn on Friday night. But her face? It was only the painted mask that came into his mind. The other face was gone, leaving only a haunting impression behind.

He stayed out in the streets until it was dark, walking and staring and searching in the dirty courts and alleys that lay behind the back of God. He was like a man who senses he has lost something of great value, but does not know for certain what it was or where he lost it. So he searches every inch of ground he's passed, not daring to return home, partly because he does not want to abandon the chance of recovering his loss, and partly because he is frightened to confirm something that might have been only in his imagination.

Martin was morbidly afraid of facing his nurse in case she saw in his face the change he dreaded had come over him.

'Where ha' ye been, master?' she asked, greeting him with some relief when at last he returned to the vicarage. 'I heard ye was taken queer. Why didna' ye come straight back?'

'I – I walked, Mrs Jackson. I needed to clear my head.

It was so hot at the inquest. But I'm quite well now. Have you – have you anyone waiting to see me?'

'I sent them away, master. Just as soon as I heard ye wasna' yourself.'

'Not myself?'

'Poorly, I meant.'

'I – I wish you hadn't sent them away. I might have been of some help to them, you know ... I – I was quite looking forward to it ... after the courtroom!'

He gave a forced laugh, but Mrs Jackson shook her head sagely.

'I've known ye since ye was a bairn, master; and I can see you're tired out.'

'Like your St Peter of Hoy? Do I look as if I'd been wrestling with the devil, Mrs Jackson?'

'You puir soul, to be thinking on such things! It's your eyes, master. That's where it always shows. You'd best be up to bed.'

'All the same, I wish you hadn't sent those people away.'

'Why! You'd be no gude to yourself or them!'

'Why should you say such a thing? Why should you say that I'd be no good to people you know I could have helped? You always said that I'd only to come into a room and – bring comfort. Why not now? Why should tiredness have made me different? I could just have gone in to see them. What made you say that it would do no good?'

She stared at him curiously, but did not answer; so he went up to bed, bitterly regretting his insistence on what, after all, had only been a figure of speech.

He lay on his bed without undressing and stared at the ceiling. His homecoming had filled him with unutterable dismay. What if it really was so – that because of his guilt in concealing the murder, his talent, his gift, had been destroyed?

But why should that be? He'd lied many times in his childhood and youth and sinned as often as the opportunity offered; and his gift had never suffered. Sometimes it had seemed the very reverse, as if his mysterious power was a plant that thrived on a dunghill. He remembered his father's death-bed, and the look of grateful peace in response to the pressure of Martin's hand. Yet that hand, he recollected, biting his lip, had still been warm from fondling the breast of his mother's maid.

The pallid face of Dr Dormann rose before him, and the force of inexplicable hatred that emanated from it struck him like a blow. What if there really were such things as his superstitious nurse insisted, and the man from the Mulberry Garden was some sort of devil and the girl was the ancient temptress sent into the garden to destroy him? He tried again to remember her face, but could not. All that came to him was a feeling of tenderness that he could not suppress. The very fact that he had been unable to find her made her curiously precious. *Now the serpent was more subtle than any beast of the field.* Had the devil prevailed over him so completely that he had been brought to love the cause of his ruin?

Or was it that the murdered youth himself had pleaded in another court for justice against the priest who condemned him to rot in the earth unavenged? *Vengeance is mine; I will repay, saith the Lord.* Martin shut his eyes in anguish as these fantastic thoughts thronged his brain. His was not an introspective mind; it was more apt to flicker rapidly from scene to scene, sensing and responding rather than inquiring into the logic or meaning of them.

Suddenly he stood up, as another thought struck him. He had hidden the evidence of his own guilt in the church.

That was monstrous! He must remove it at once! And then he must pray for forgiveness for such an act of desecration.

He waited for what must have been half an hour, listening intently until he was certain the household was asleep; then he crept from his room like a thief . . .

The church was fathoms deep in darkness, and the long pews slumbered through sermons of silence. He made his way quickly to the vestry and began to rummage in the drawer where he had hidden the piece of cloth.

He could not find it. At once he flew into a panic that someone had forestalled him and stolen it. With trembling hands he lit a candle – and found the piece of cloth almost at once. In the haste of his search it had dropped on the floor.

He went back into the body of the church, still carrying the candle. The pillars that flanked the aisles rushed and streamed in the unsteady light like naked trees in a wind. He cupped his hand round the flame and it was as if huge black wings had suddenly swept into the building and were beating noiselessly over his head.

He shivered, then entered the first pew and knelt down, placing the candle carefully beside him. He prayed, with all the strength he had, to be forgiven for what he had done . . . and then unconsciously looked up towards the altar, as if for some sign that his prayer had been answered. But the altar was hidden in shadows and he had to raise the candle to dispel them.

He stared painfully at the place from where he was accustomed to approach his God. It was blank and empty. Nothing moved there; no voice spoke to him.

He begged, he pleaded for a sign that his prayer had been heard. In doing so, he remembered all the tales his nurse had told him of women, fair as flowers, of blazing

69

infants and swords of light appearing before saints in glens, on mountain sides and rising up from the fishermen's sea. He did not aspire to be granted a miracle on such a scale; all he wanted was to be vouchsafed an inner kindling – a *sense* of forgiveness.

As he gazed at the altar he saw the light of his candle reflected in the gilded candlesticks; for a moment it seemed as if the laws of nature were suspended and the tall, pale altar candles were burning upside down. He shook his head; to take an illusion for a sign would be to deny *everything*.

He took the piece of cloth from his pocket and examined it in the candlelight. One corner had been soaked with blood that had dried and turned blackish. The patterning was of small yellow stars on a grey muslin sky. It was curious that he'd thought they were flowers before.

He held it over the flame till his fingers began to burn with the heat. The muslin began to smoke, then to smoulder. Suddenly it flared up and Martin dropped it with a cry of dismay. The interior of the church shook and reddened from the little conflagration; then Martin trod it out and the smell of burning cloth was everywhere.

He bent down to recover what he could; but it was unrecognizable. He hadn't meant to burn it. He swore to God he hadn't meant to. Rather had he meant to burn and blister his own fingers, as if reliving a dream of childhood when he, the infant saint, roasted on the kitchen spit.

He blew out the candle and backed away towards the church door. He stopped. He had heard something: a sigh, a sound of breathing. He was not alone. Somewhere someone was hiding, watching him. He stared into the corners and then, one by one, along the dark pews. He was hideously afraid.

In the last pew he saw something black, huddled on the

bench. He crept close, half expecting the black shape to stand up and confront him with the face of Dr Dormann. But it didn't move. He stared down upon it. It was a child, a street urchin, sleeping, or pretending to sleep.

Shaking with fear and guilt, Martin left the church. What if the child had heard him and seen him? Or worse! What if the child had been no child at all, but the sign he had prayed for? And the answer was: there is no escape, not even in the church. Burn what you will, you cannot hide your guilt from the watchers.

Chapter Eight

THE following morning began dull and heavy, and the sun rose somewhere in gloomy secrecy. At ten o'clock, the vicarage received a visitor who did nothing to improve the weather. Martin's mother called.

'There's no need to look so terrified, Martin,' she began briskly, even before her son could greet her. 'I've not come to stay. I'm putting up with my friends in Hanover Square.'

She laid a slight emphasis on 'friends', and accompanied it with a meaning glance towards Mrs Jackson whom she had never forgiven for filling her son's head with nonsense.

'I only called because I was in Town and I am your mother, after all.' Another look at Mrs Jackson who retreated towards the back of the hall.

'Will you take breakfast, mother?' asked Martin uneasily. His mother's presence, and the feeling of discord she always seemed to radiate, unsettled him profoundly.

'Tea,' said Mrs Young firmly. 'Only tea. Otherwise just a glass of water. I don't want to put anyone out. I imagine that you are far too busy these days to see that your servants look after the household properly.'

'We have tea, ma'am,' said Mrs Jackson quietly, and retired to the kitchen.

Feebly Martin attempted to defend his old nurse, but Mrs Young was adamant.

'That woman has always been your evil genius, Martin. It's all her fault that you are as you are – a stranger to your family. Do you never spare a thought for me, buried in the country with your brother, when I might have had a younger son whom I could visit with pleasure and pride? Look at you, Martin! Pale as a ghost and living like a monk! Why don't you get married, at least, and live a normal life? There must be any number of pretty girls with money who'd jump at the chance of being Mrs Martin Young!'

Martin sighed wearily. He knew perfectly well that his mother only wanted him to get married in order to supplant the influence of Mrs Jackson. He led the way into the breakfast parlour and Mrs Young drank her tea, complaining only that it was a little too hot. Presently she set down her cup and leaned across the table with brightly inquiring eyes. She was still a fine-looking woman . . .

'There was something I wanted to ask you, dear. I was thinking about it only this morning. That murder in the little pleasure garden near here. Everybody's talking about it. You are the magistrate, aren't you, who's looking into it?'

Martin smiled bitterly as he guessed that the only reason for his mother's visit was to obtain a little more news than her friends about the fashionable crime.

'They say a woman did it. Have you caught her yet? What a scandal it would be if she turns out to be a respectably married woman! And the young man she stabbed; was he really as beautiful as everyone says? Some day you must take me to this garden of yours. I'd like to see it, you know. Now tell me, Martin – have you any suspicions? I promise to be discreet . . .'

His mother's face was alive with unwholesome curiosity. She looked ugly and lascivious, and unfamiliar. He shrank from her.

'No . . . no! I – I have no idea.'

'There's no need to be so abrupt. What is wrong with you, Martin? There's something the matter. You don't look yourself. There's something on your mind, isn't there! Tell me, is it a woman? It always used to be, before you made up your mind – or had it made up for you – to become a saint.'

'I – I slept badly. I'm sorry if I seemed abrupt. I have to get ready now for the service.'

'May I come . . . into your church?'

Mrs Young looked suddenly pathetic as she asked her favour. Although, of her two children, she much preferred the elder, she actually had an awed regard for Martin. She really did feel that in Martin she had produced a child with an unusual gift. She herself was relatively immune to it, but there was no doubt of its effect on others. Her dislike of Mrs Jackson was largely jealousy; the servant had recognized the gift that the mother had been excluded from.

'To tell you the truth, Martin, I've not been feeling well lately. Oh don't worry! It's nothing serious. It's just that I get terribly depressed. I thought that perhaps my wonderful younger son might bring his mother some comfort for a change? Will you read the lesson?'

'Yes, of course! Of course I'll read it!'

'What is the text for today? Nothing gloomy, I hope!'

'It's the Book of Daniel; the fourth chapter. You remember: Nebuchadnezzar . . .'

Mrs Young smiled and extended her hand to her son.

He prayed silently; he pleaded that, just for this once, his gift might return to him. But the church smelled of burning; the bitter odour of burnt cloth filled his nostrils so that it seemed impossible that it could pass unnoticed. He raised his eyes and looked to the back where the child, or the image of a child, had been sleeping or pretending to sleep. No one was sitting there.

He began upon the service and came at last to the reading of the first lesson, supplanting a worthy parishioner who had practised long and hard.

'*I saw in the visions of my head upon my bed, and, behold, a watcher and an holy one came down from heaven ...*'

He looked up from the grim black print to the place at the back. It was now occupied. Dr Dormann was sitting there, watching him ... Martin staggered slightly and had to hold on to the lectern to gain his balance. He saw his mother look up, concerned. He tried to smile at her; and then returned to the text which, for an instant, was a jumble of incomprehensible marks.

He read on, haltingly, and far exceeded the number of verses required. The tale of Nebuchadnezzar and his strange dream seized his terrified imagination.

'*The tree that thou sawest, which grew, and was strong, whose height reached unto heaven ...*'

He paused and looked again to the thin, terrible doctor from the Mulberry Garden. He had gone! Had he ever been there?

He stared down at his mother, and thought he saw a touch of dismay on her face.

'*While the word was in the king's mouth,*' he read, '*there fell a voice from heaven, saying, O king Nebuchadnezzar, to thee it is spoken; The kingdom is departed from thee.*'

'The kingdom is departed from thee.' After the service, Mrs Young thanked Martin, but made no mention as to whether he had succeeded or failed in what she hoped. Instead she asked him if the Mulberry Garden was within walking distance and, if so, would he point it out to her? As she spoke, the unfamiliar, disagreeably eager look came into her eyes. Nevertheless he offered her his arm and walked with her and showed her the high, jagged-topped wall of the garden.

'Why, it's like a prison!' she exclaimed. 'Is it to keep people out – or in?'

The garden did not open until the late afternoon, so Mrs Young had to be content with a glimpse through the locked gate and reading a notice that proclaimed that on the last Friday of the month there would be a grand masquerade.

They walked back through Rag Street, just as some spots of warm, heavy rain began to fall. Martin looked round for shelter; they were standing outside a milliner's establishment, conducted by one Mrs Gish, late of Bond Street. In the window was displayed a cape of rose velvet. He stared at it, in the grip of countless memories, then, on an impulse, said:

'Do you remember that cape of yours I spoiled?'

His mother laughed. 'I do indeed! But I've forgiven you for that!'

'Let me buy you another now!'

'Don't be absurd, Martin!'

'It's beginning to rain. Look! There's a fine cape there! Please let me buy it for you!'

'My dear son . . . in a place like this? Really, Martin . . . Besides, it's not my colour. I won't have you wasting your money! No – no! Another time . . .'

Although she protested, it was evident that she was deeply moved by Martin's offer and the intention, she felt, that lay behind it. As they stood arguing the rain increased and Mrs Gish, late of Bond Street, stood watching them with her hand upon the door. At length she judged the time ripe and stepped outside: a neat, shining woman who might have been carved out of solid satin.

'Can I be of assistance?' she inquired, and then, affecting just to recognize Martin, curtsied stiffly and added: 'Your Reverence!'

'That cape in the window. I would like to buy it for this lady.'

'If modom would come inside?'

'No – no! I really don't want to. It was a ridiculous idea!'

'There is no obligation, modom. But if we was just to try on the garment?'

'Oh very well! Martin! I'm very cross with you! And I told you, it's not my colour!'

They were ushered into a dingy showroom that stank of stale scent and was painted red, like the inside of an old mouth. Mrs Young looked expressively at her son who, however, was quite unrepentant. The cape was fetched and Mrs Young tried it on. She stalked up and down, flirting with the two mirrors in a helplessly absorbed way. In spite of herself, she liked the cape.

'Well, Martin?' she said. 'What do you think of it now?'

Martin nodded without replying.

'Modom's brother has made a very good choice,' said Mrs Gish.

'Brother? Good heavens, he's my son!'

'No! I could see there was a resemblance ... but modom looks so youthful in the garment! I can hardly believe it! Your son?'

'Nonsense, Mrs Gish! But, as my son insists, I will take the cape. But see here ... the lining is coming unstitched! Is there anybody in your workroom who can attend to it now?'

'Of course, modom.'

She left the showroom and could be heard bawling

down a flight of steps to someone in the basement. Presently she returned, smiling exquisitely.

'The chits of girls one has to put up with these days! Even in Bond Street, as modom must know, things ain't much better. Ah! Here she comes at last. Her ladyship. Fanny! Fanny Bush! Take this cape and stitch the lining proper. And be sharp about it.'

It was the girl from the Mulberry Garden; the young murderess herself!

She saw his look of amazed recognition, and at once an expression of terror came into her eyes, as if begging him to say nothing.

*

By the time they left the milliner's the rain had ceased, but the sky still threatened.

'That girl,' said Mrs Young. 'Didn't she remind you of that maid I had once?'

Martin shook his head. He was in a state of great agitation. He had managed to snatch a word with the girl; he had asked when he could see her. She answered instantly: 'Friday. In the garden. *Please* don't say anything now!'

'She might have been her sister,' went on Mrs Young.

'We'd better walk more quickly, mother,' said Martin; 'before the storm breaks.'

They reached the vicarage just as the rain came down again, and this time with grimmer purpose.

'Look, Jackson!' exclaimed Mrs Young. 'Look what my son has bought me!'

And she paraded herself in her new cape with childish pleasure, while, outside, scissors of lightning split the clouds open and the heavens roared.

Chapter Nine

MRS GISH's was the premier establishment in Rag Street, being the only one that dealt in new clothing; otherwise the thoroughfare was the proud man's nightmare and the philosopher's delight, where the former might see his cast-offs exhibited with their every patch and shameful stain exposed, and the latter might meditate on the fate of human vanity and how the first fig-leaf, put on out of shame, had become an ingenious fantasy of worm-spun self-esteem.

Two doors away from Mrs Gish's was a dealer in battered buttons where Martin had visited when the scarlet fever struck. He called again and, in passing, inquired about the girl who sewed for Mrs Gish.

It had seemed to him a sign and a miracle that he had found the girl, and he almost smiled at his childish and superstitious fears that she'd been the ancient temptress, conjured out of air to steal his soul away.

The lady of the house was everyone's neighbour, and knew about half as much as God; and whatever had escaped her she made up out of a fund of experience, gleaned from the purchase and sale of buttons.

The girl's name was Fanny Bush and she'd been with Mrs Gish for something over a year. The exact time was available if His Reverence desired. She was, as girls went, a hard worker; and Mrs Gish took advantage. She was reasonably polite, but once or twice – the walls being thin – she'd been heard to have a tongue in her head and to have known words unfitting to her sex and age. Although she was not on the streets, it was only a matter of time before she came to it, as she was an extravagant puss with notions above her station. For instance, she'd taken a fancy to a ragged old fellow, old enough to be her grand-dad, and spent money on him like water, sometimes even cooking up a meal for him in her basement room and smelling the neighbourhood out with cabbage and onions. And her with hardly a penny to bless herself with! On such occasions, she wouldn't even give you the time of day, being so puffed up with being the lady of charity. She would have been better advised to spend her money on making something of herself, rather than trusting to providence and her looks – which certainly wouldn't last.

'But taken all in all,' finished up the button-dealer's wife, 'I've known worse than her. At least, she keeps herself to herself.' Which, thought Martin, involuntarily, was surprising in view of how much had been discovered about her.

'She's not in any sort of trouble, I hope?' asked the lady with interest. 'I wouldn't like to think that of her.'

'No . . . no. It's just that she – she reminded me of somebody.'

It was impossible for Martin to wait until Friday. He had to see her before that. The long and aching search had created in him such a feeling of urgency that he haunted Rag Street whenever he could in the frail hope that the girl would emerge, however briefly.

On the Thursday he waited opposite, long after it had grown dark, and watched the light reflected from her basement room, while night-children scuttled up and down the street like insects and stung him with their eyes.

At last he heard the basement door open and then close. He heard footsteps on the stone steps. Eagerly he crossed the street – in time to come face to face with the ragged old man who was wiping his greasy mouth and clutching a bag of fruit.

At once a look of utter terror came into the old man's face. He dropped his bag, which had contained oranges, and fled. Martin stared after him in amazement.

'Your oranges!' he called out. 'You've dropped them!' The old man cast a wild look over his shoulder, but did not stop. Martin bent to gather up the fruit, but, out of nowhere, an urchin with a face like a walnut swooped and forestalled him.

He stood up and began to walk after the old man, who was now no more than a hobbling shadow in Townsend Lane. He meant to give the old man some money to make up his loss, for which Martin felt partly responsible. Also he was consumed with curiosity as to why he had looked terrified. He had looked like a criminal, detected in the very commission of his crime.

He followed him into Vine Street and then across Saffron Hill. From time to time he paused and glared desperately behind him, but his old eyes were never sharp enough to see his pursuer. Whenever he stopped, Martin stepped into a doorway and waited till the old man went on again. Where was he going in such fear and haste?

At length they came to Hatton Garden and the old man relaxed his pace. He began to walk along by the diamond merchants' great houses until, suddenly, he vanished.

With a feeling of bewildered unreality, Martin approached the place; to his relief he discovered a dark cleft between two of the houses that led to a quiet, enclosed courtyard. At the further end hung a single lantern in the portico of a stone-built house. There was no sign of the old man, but the lantern was still swinging as if the substantial front door had just been shut.

He hesitated for a moment, and then crossed the court-yard and knocked on the door. Almost at once a servant in livery answered.

'The old man,' began Martin, his feeling of unreality increasing, for the portico under which he stood reminded him of a well-kept tomb.

'Your name, sir?' asked the servant.

Martin produced a card which the servant scrutinized with an air of faint incredulity, as if he found it hard to credit that the distracted young gentleman and the name on the card belonged together.

'The old man,' repeated Martin urgently, 'who just came in here! I want to see him.'

'I will take your card in to my master,' said the servant and, consulting the card again, added: 'Your Reverence.'

'But it's not your master I want to see! It was that shabby old man who just this moment came in.'

'Yes, sir. My master,' said the servant. 'Sir David Brown. Do you still wish to see him?'

Although the words were polite, the tone implied: 'Don't you think it a shame that a fine upstanding young fellow like me should be working for an old wretch like him who's not worth an undertaker's candle?' He cocked his head on one side and looked at Martin inquiringly.

'I – I don't understand,' muttered Martin, passing his hand across his forehead. 'The old man I meant was shabby and poor . . . a beggar almost . . .'

'If you will step inside, Your Reverence, I will take in your card.'

The hall was richly furnished; but it felt cold, as if the stone-built house enclosed a changeless winter. The servant departed, and presently Martin heard voices, one low and yielding, the other querulous and distinctly aggrieved.

'No! No! I won't see him! Tell him I'm not at home!'

'But sir . . . Reverend . . . Justice . . . saw you . . .'

'I don't care! Send him away! Who is master here? Tell him I've just gone out!'

'Very well, sir . . .'

The servant returned to the hall with the slightest of nods towards the room he had just left. He had neglected to close the door.

'My master,' he murmured blandly, 'is not at home.' He cocked his head towards the open door, as if to say: Look for yourself. I really wish you would. It would serve him right – the old scoundrel!

'Pardon me, Your Reverence,' he said suddenly, cupping his hand in an exaggerated fashion to his ear. 'I think I hear my lady calling.'

He bowed and departed with the most expressive of glances towards his recalcitrant master.

Martin waited, not a little repelled by the contempt and hostility that seemed to exist in the cold mansion. At length he shrugged his shoulders and opened the front door. He paused on the threshold. He really ought to wait for the servant to return. He closed the door. At once, the querulous voice demanded:

'Has he gone yet?'

'No, sir!' said Martin, helplessly smiling at the success of his unwitting deception. 'I am still waiting to see you.'

Instantly the door the servant had left ajar slammed shut. Martin approached it.

'Sir David!'

'Go away! Go away! I won't see you!'

'Why not, sir? What are you frightened of?'

Martin found himself becoming angry at the old man's extraordinary and childish behaviour.

'I'm not frightened! Why have you followed me here?'

'You dropped your fruit. Why did you run away?'

'I didn't! I didn't!'

'Were you so ashamed of being caught coming out of Fanny Bush's room? Was that it?'

There was a sound like a sob; the door opened and the old man, his face like death, beckoned Martin into the room.

'Don't go shouting it all over the house!'

He shut the door and retreated into a high-backed chair that stood by the empty fireplace. He crouched in the seat with his hands pressed between his grubby, threadbare knees, and glared malevolently up at Martin.

'So you know her!'

'Yes. And I know that she feeds you and gives you money. And I know that you are a rich man. How can you let her pity you?'

'I don't! I don't!' His invariable defence was to deny everything.

'Then she knows you are rich?'

The wretched old man did not answer; he sat rigidly in his throne-like chair, gnawing his lip. At length he mumbled defiantly:

'I've not committed a crime. There's no law I've broken. There's no need for you to stand there looking down on me like a judge and jury. I won't be judged, I tell you!'

'Not by me,' said Martin, feeling sickened by the old man. He backed away, when the old man cried out:

'And God won't judge me, either! It's in the Bible! "*Now King David*" (that's me!) "*was old and stricken in years; and they covered him with clothes, but he gat no heat.*" (D'you see? D'you see?) "*Wherefore his servants said unto him, let there be sought for my lord a young virgin: and let her stand before the king, and let her cherish him, and let her lie in thy bosom, that my lord the king might get heat.*"'

He had reeled off the verses at panting speed, then peered up at Martin with a look of horrible cunning. He beckoned Martin towards him and suddenly reached forward and clutched him by the wrist.

'Feel me!' he moaned, piteously. 'Am I not cold? Don't you see that I'm freezing to death?'

He released Martin's wrist and thrust his hand back between his knees.

'Don't tell her, *please*! Swear to God you won't tell her!'

'I don't understand –'

As abruptly as he'd put it on, the old man abandoned his piteous manner and the angry malevolence returned.

'You're like the rest of them in this house! You don't understand! And if that girl knew I was rich, she wouldn't understand, either! But God has let her pity me! That's a

feeling; and feelings are warm, my fine young friend. And I am freezing to death! Ah! I can read the look on your face! Here's an old man who ought to know better! Age brings wisdom and all that claptrap! Well, let me tell you, I'm past philosophy, Your Reverence! I've been right through it and I'm out on the other side! It's the Bible for me now. "*And the damsel was very fair, and cherished the king, and ministered to him* . . ." That's what it comes down to . . . that's what's remembered: the warmth, the old swallowing warmth!'

He clutched himself in mournful secrecy, and Martin stared blindly down upon him in all his terrible nakedness. The deeper one looked into a man, the shallower he became. All wit, cleverness and learning vanished away like the writing on a slate, till nothing was left but a need for warmth.

'*Please* don't tell her.'

Martin shuddered, but made no answer.

'I've paid, you know. I've paid for my warmth.'

'How?'

'Look. My ticket . . . my season ticket. I paid a hundred pounds.'

He dragged something out of his coat pocket and showed it to Martin. It was a pewter medallion, engraved with a mulberry tree.

'What does it mean?'

'It's for the Mulberry Garden. Dr Dormann promised me that if I paid up, Fanny Bush would never be told about me and that I'd be left in peace. He gave me his word. We shook hands on it. He *promised*.'

'*Dr Dormann?*' The name struck terror into his heart. Since the inquest he had walked in dread of the time when the man would confront him.

'Yes. Dr Dormann. A strange, strange man. I thought he was the devil at first; but afterwards I saw he was different. When we shook hands I knew he was a saint. *He* understood. I love the Mulberry Garden . . . I love the Mulberry Garden . . .'

On the Friday night Martin entered the Mulberry Garden to keep his appointment with the murderess. The gatekeeper took his shilling and wished him a pleasant evening.

He walked along the tunnelled paths that skirted the high wall as if afraid to approach the heart of the garden and the kingdom of Dr Dormann.

As he walked, he became aware of murmurs and soft laughter everywhere. This part of the garden was unfamiliar to him; most likely it was near where the murder had been committed. He passed under an arch of tangled roses, and saw a fragment of lace hanging from a thorn.

He stopped to examine it, half expecting to find it blood-stained.

He left the path and began to traverse a shrubbery where the bushes shivered and the night seemed to twitch in petticoats. Snatches of faces turned to stare after him incuriously, then vanished into dark clouds of hair. He saw a flash of naked limbs . . . and looked away, feeling that he was not the watcher but the watched. The trees were full of eyes . . .

Presently he came to the great pit where the lake was to be. He could see faintly (there were no lanterns near) the roots of trees protruding from the torn sides of earth. They were like skinless hands, murdered in the act of grasping.

He stood staring into the pit till the hands began to move and dark shapes began to roll and slither in the depths.

'Come down, come down!' voices called inside his head. 'Come down into the dark with us! We are the spirits of the garden!'

'No, no! I am Saint Martin of Clerkenwell!'

'We will give you back your talent, your gift!'

'My gift was from God.'

'That's right, that's right! We are the children of God. Dr Dormann has your gift. He is a saint who brings comfort and peace to freezing old men. He sees all and forgives all . . .'

'Even murder?'

'There are worse things than murder.'

'What?'

'The cold . . . cold . . . cold . . .'

Martin put his hands to his ears to shut out the satanic voices. When he took his hands away, he heard the sound of laughter. For a moment he thought it came from the trees themselves; but then he decided that it came from the shrubbery where lovers were tumbling in the dark. He left the pit filled with foreboding, and went to keep his appointment.

Chapter Ten

THE child Briskitt laughed aloud – a weird, disembodied sound like the excitement of bats. Cradled in thorns, the companion of beetles and earwigs, he peered down through his spy-hole in the twelfth arbour at the couple in the dark. They were at it like a pair of pigeons – all wings and flutter and jumping beaks. You couldn't help but laugh.

'What was that?' asked Leila Robinson.

'Insects!' panted Major Smith. 'It's just like it was in Bombay.'

Briskitt stifled his natural merriment and, with straight face, crooked limbs and undecipherable brain, began to descend from his nest. The tendril of a vine snapped with a noise like a pistol shot.

'What was that?'

'What? What is it now?'

'Something cracked.'

'Joints,' said Major Smith ruefully. 'Bombay and *anno Domini*, my dear . . .'

'What a pretty name,' said Miss Robinson. 'You must miss her something dreadful.'

Briskitt touched the ground and then, noiseless as a dream child, he went in search of Chops. Presently he found him out in his fastness, so basketed with twigs that he resembled a child half bewitched to wood.

'Meetcha in the 'ole!' mouthed Briskitt.

Chops's eyes acknowledged his patron's claims upon him, and Briskitt departed to lurk in the nethermost part of the lake pit, where Wednesday's rain still lingered and made a pudding of mud.

Briskitt's financial empire was spreading and he had need of a satrap to administer a province of it. In short, he had reached the melancholy conclusion that he could not be in two places at once and that Chops would have to deputize for him, and follow the Reverend Martin Young while he, Briskitt, met with his mysterious acquaintance of the previous Friday . . . the goose of the golden eggs.

The following of Martin Young from the garden was a task laid upon him by Dr Dormann and had brought in many a sixpence. It was a task that might safely be deputed to Chops. After all, what were friends for?

Thoughtfully he lifted a beetle out of a puddle and helped it to safety; then he frowned. What would he really do if his income ceased? Perhaps unwisely (but then, what fortunes are ever made wisely?), he had invested every penny he possessed in property. He had bought himself a peach of a waistcoat (that would fit him by and by), and a model ship he'd long coveted. As yet, he had not sailed this vessel, as the only water he'd found had been so wide and windy that he'd been mortally terrified his property would be blown out of reach. Thus the child Briskitt was already prey to the fearful heartache that is the bane of capitalism. Moodily he stared across the dark pit and wondered when they'd get a move on and fill it up with lake.

The remainder of his capital had been sunk into a silver chain and locket into which he'd managed to insinuate a twist of his rat's-tail hair. He intended it to be a keepsake for 'our ma'.

He beamed. Already Chops had conveyed to him the lady's undying gratitude for favours received; the natural son having informed him with awe that his parent had been able to purchase gin in sufficient quantities to lay her out cold for a day. 'And she ain't no beginner!' Chops had added, by way of tribute. Also she had bought a knitted shawl and a pair of shoes, nearly new.

'You'd be that proud at the sight of her!' Chops had said.

'Tell 'er it's nothin' . . . nothin' to wot's to come!'

'She said to give you a great big 'ug'nakiss,' said Chops, doubtfully.

'Tell our ma,' Briskitt had answered, holding up a hand to ward off the threatened embrace, 'that I'll come an' claim it meself!'

The beetle had fallen into the puddle again. Briskitt sighed and lifted it out. He was to bestow the keepsake and claim his 'ug'nakiss this very night; he felt tender towards everything.

Briskitt looked up and compressed his lips. Chops was coming down like a bleeding landslide. When he arrived, Briskitt punched him sharply in the ribs.

'What's that for?'

'You gone an' squashed my beetle. 'S under yer foot.'

Guiltily Chops removed his foot from the remains, and inquired how he might serve his patron. Briskitt told him, twisting his ear from time to time by way of subtly emphasizing the need for integrity and discretion.

Chops rubbed his ear. 'Where are *you* going, Briskitt?'

'Business,' answered Briskitt.

'You're going to get some more of that money what you got last Friday.'

Briskitt offered no comment.

'I'd tell *you*, Briskitt,' pursued Chops, with a touch of resentment.

'Well I ain't tellin' *you*.'

'I hopes nobody sticks a knife in *you*, Briskitt,' said Chops, preparing to depart. 'I reely hopes they don't.'

'Whyjer say that?' demanded Briskitt, raising a threatening fist.

"Cause of last Friday. I ain't so silly as I look, Briskitt.'

'Piss off!' said Briskitt, savagely; and huddled himself down in the mud. Chops had quite unnerved him.

The gaiety of the rotunda sounded faint and disjointed as Briskitt lurked in the pit, watchful and apprehensive. He was in a bitter mood. His high expectations had been undermined by the very infant he had honoured with his protection and regard. The seed of fear had been planted and it flourished like the bay tree. He started and clenched his fists.

'Izzat you?'

'Yes. I promised.'

"Old on. I'll come up.'

'I can climb down –'

'No. Don't fancy you an' me down 'ere in the dark.'

'Are you frightened? What do you think I'd do?'

'Never you mind!'

'I wouldn't harm you.'

'You won't get the bleedin' chance!'

'You're only a little boy –'

'None o' that! I'm the one wot saw! There's no one else.'

'You've kept your word?'

"Course I 'ave!' (A touch of pride and indignation denoted that Briskitt had his standards.)

'Here! Here's the money, then.'

'Wot? Only three?'

'Better than nothing, you little bloodsucker!'

'You're a fine 'un to talk abaht blood!'

'All right, all right! I'll try to bring more next Friday.'

'That's better. I didn't mean to upset you. It's jus' that I got me future to think abaht. I got 'sponsibilities.'

93

'Of course you have!'

'Don't you worry. I won't let on, even though I could 'ave pissed meself laughing.'

'Why?'

'When they was all lookin' for 'is coat.'

'His coat?'

'Yes. You remember abaht 'is coat.'

'Oh yes, yes . . . His coat –'

'See you nex' Fridy.'

'Here? In the . . . pit?'

'There's nowhere else in the garden wot's safe.'

'The garden! What sort of a nightmare is it? What does it grow on?'

'Cockle shells an' silver bells an' pretty maids all in a row!'

Chapter Eleven

THERE she sat – the young lady of charity – laughing in
the lantern light at a table not far from the rotunda. She
wore a straw hat and a grubby white gown all spotted
with tiny red flowers as if she'd walked under a war of
sparrows and got caught in a shower of their blood. Beside
her sat the old wretch, Sir David Brown, crumbling up
cake and stuffing it into his mouth. From time to time
Fanny Bush leaned over and patted his sleeve, then pointed
to the singer or some group who'd caught her fancy.
She'd murmur something and laugh, and the old man
would nod and smile most piteously.

Imperiously she summoned a waiter, gave him an order
and then looked round proudly, as if to say: 'Think what
you like! This is my pleasure – this is my night!'

Martin watched her as her eyes traversed the path
round the mulberry tree, lighting eagerly on each fresh
stroller as he came into view. Her glance lingered for a
moment on the remains of the chalked cross where Isaac
Fisk had died; then something else attracted her and she
laughed again.

Could she, like the old man at her side, have sold herself
to Dr Dormann and been absolved from memory and
guilt? Martin looked round at the other revellers, familiar
faces all, who clustered like flies round the gleaming
rotunda, while Orpheus Jones poured forth the treacle of
his voice. What if they were all caught in the web of the
garden?

All his old superstitious fears returned till the garden's
many perfumes seemed stifling. The voices from the pit
dinned in his ears again as he walked towards the murder-

ess. What if he was really setting out to wrestle with God and not with the devil? What if this garden was all that there was left of the Garden of Eden and it was he who was bringing the knowledge of sin into it?

The girl had seen him. She smiled nervously and half waved. She said something to the old man, who stared at him, at first defiantly and then with a horrible, sick panic. He mumbled to the girl and got up to go. She tried to restrain him. He shook his head violently. Much troubled, she pressed some money into his hand. He took it, and, with a last look of dread and hatred at Martin, fled.

'Why did you do that?' she asked angrily, as Martin approached. 'Why did you frighten Mr Brown away? It's his night, you know, just as much as yours.'

Martin hesitated. He did not want to betray the old man's secret.

'What did he say?'

'That he didn't want to see you.'

'Perhaps he has a guilty conscience.'

'What can he have done? Poor old man!'

'Perhaps he's ashamed.'

'He's no call to be. He can't help being old and poor.'

Martin compressed his lips, but said nothing. The girl looked away with an air of indifference, much at odds with her panic-stricken look when she'd seen him in Mrs Gish's shop.

'*Love in her eyes sits playing,*' sang Orpheus Jones and a voice from a nearby table, where murder still lingered in the mind, remembered:

'I can see him now. All that blood coming out over his shirt . . .'

'*And sheds delicious death . . .*'

'You might as well have his cake,' said Fanny Bush remotely. 'No sense in wasting it.'

'Love on her lips is straying . . .'

('Do you believe in ghosts? I dreamed about him every night . . . just coming round the path, there . . . and pointing at –')

'Suit yourself. I'll give it to the birds.'

'And warbling in her breath.'

('Do you think they'll ever find her? I don't like to think of a woman being hanged . . .')

'You can sit down if you like.'

'Love on her breast sits panting –'

('They say it's worse than a man. They say their insides fall out . . .')

'And swells with soft desire!'

'Aren't you well, or something?'

Martin made a gigantic effort to disentangle himself from the web of inconsequential words.

'I'm all right, thank you.'

He gazed down at the girl from the garden and was filled with an aching desire to help her and save her, no matter what the cost. In the confused and shadowy lantern light, she seemed to dissolve into his mother's maid and many another like her who'd filled the hectic years before he'd sold himself to God.

'I'm sorry I spoke so sharp,' she said, smiling suddenly. 'It was just that I couldn't see why old Mr Brown should have been so frightened of you. You don't frighten me at all. You never have. Everyone says you're very kind and have got a real gift for bringing comfort where it's needed. It's true, you know. I didn't believe it, but it's true. I've forgotten all about being angry. I feel quite happy now.' She paused, and then added quietly, 'By the way, thank you for not saying anything in front of Mrs Gish. About last Friday, I mean.'

'I wanted to talk to you . . .'

'Well? Here I am.'

'Not here. This place seems all eyes and ears ... Will you walk with me?'

'The garden's closing any minute.'

'Outside, then?'

'I got to go straight back.'

'I'll walk with you . . .'

She looked at him with a sudden, unfathomable expression that made his heart contract. He felt excited and frightened. The girl stood up; he offered her his arm and together they began to stroll from the rotunda. Martin looked back and, for one brief moment, the whole green and spotted gold fabric, with its dancing shadows, its bright faces and its dark sky, *everything* seemed to part like a curtain and the vast face of Dr Dormann peered through. Then it swung back, and all was real again, with not a crack or a seam anywhere.

They walked down the winding paths and presently out of the garden's gate. A moment later there slipped out after them a diminutive shadow, like the ghost of a rat . . .

Rag Street was empty, save for the odd scraps of night children who scampered and scuttled, making free of their kingdom of the night.

They're like mice, thought Martin, bred in darkness to inhabit the holes and skirtings everywhere. He frowned and put them from his mind . . .

The girl had relinquished his arm as if, once out of the garden, a gulf had opened between them. They walked a foot apart, careful of cracks and rifts in the pavement, and watched by headless liveries and old dead gowns that dimly crowded the battered shop windows. A tarnished suit (property of a bankrupt), with wrinkled breeches and pockets grinning like toothless mouths, smirked and bowed with a kind of greasy knowingness, as if to say: 'We all come to it in the end. We all pass from the new to the shameless secondhand.'

'This is where I live,' said Fanny suddenly. 'Thank you for seeing me home.' And then, as an afterthought, added: 'Sir.'

With a start Martin realized he had not uttered a single word since they'd left the garden. The task he had set himself seemed superhuman and altogether beyond his strength; his tongue refused to utter what his mind urged, and he could only stand, staring into the girl's hauntingly pretty face. She held out her hand – when suddenly there was a hiss and a scuttle and an infant, not much bigger than a dog, shot between them and vanished into the dark as if he'd been discharged from a gun.

'They're always round you!' said Fanny with a smile. 'Do you like children?'

'Yes . . . yes. I suppose so.'

'They must notice it, too. Your gift, I mean. It *is* a gift, and it's got nothing to do with your being a clergyman or anything like that.'

Martin's heart began to beat rapidly as wild hopes rose up in his mind and sent his thoughts racing.

'I still have it, then?'

'You do for me,' said Fanny simply. 'If they was all like you, I might even go to church. Not,' she added hastily, 'that there's anything particularly holy about you. It's just that I like being with you. You've got a wicked pair of eyes, you know,' she said with a burst of mischievousness.

Martin bit his lip and looked away.

'I wanted to ask you something . . . about last Friday.'

'I've got to go now. I'm late.'

'Can I come in with you?'

'I – I'd sooner you didn't.'

'Please.'

'Last Friday . . . I didn't mean it, you know.'

What was it she didn't mean? The killing – or the offer she'd made him?

'I know that,' he said.

'All right, then. But don't make any noise. I'm not allowed followers.'

She opened the iron gate, which screamed like a soul in hell, and led the way down the stone steps in front of the shop.

She lived in the basement front, and, as she lit a candle, Mrs Gish's voice bawled down from aloft:

'Who's there?'

'Me, ma'am! Fanny!'

'Dirty little stop-out! Who's that you've brought back?'

'Only the vicar, ma'am! He's come for Evensong!'

'None of your sauce, miss!'

'Silly old cow! Go hang yourself in your garters!'

'What was that?'

'I said – did you want me to put out a card for the carter's?'

She shut the door of her room and turned to Martin, glowing with delight over her victorious battle of wits. Her face, in the candlelight, looked wild and exultant, and for an instant resembled the expression on Dr Dormann's face as he'd watched Martin damn himself at the inquest. Then she put the candle down and she was Fanny Bush again, brushing past him with a whiff of femininity to draw the curtains. Her little room danced and flickered all round her in the yellow light; garments in varying stages of stitching hung from pegs round the walls; shawls, caps with streamers and capes with limp hoods, like girls with broken necks, crowded the eye and suffocated the mind.

'It was just that I was skint,' she said, offering Martin

the only chair and seating herself on the bed. 'Last Friday. My friend – old Mr Brown – came over all queer; so I gave him all I had to go and see a doctor. Poor old devil! I just didn't think to keep anything back. Then two girls I know – they live near here and go on the street when they're skint – told me I ought to make something out of myself. They did up my face and dosed me with gin. You need it, first time. They said it was easy as falling asleep; and anyway, it was in the garden, not on the street.'

'And . . . did you?'

She looked at him; her eyes grew enormous – fathoms beyond conjecture. The angry pity he'd felt when he'd heard how she had offered herself as a whore for the sake of the old scoundrel who was deceiving her vanished. She was measurelessly above his pity. There was an essence about her, an actual perfume that his whole being savoured, so that to pity her would have been like pitying a meadow of flowers for the assaults of bees . . . Whatever she did was touched with the grace of –

'And did I what?' she added, smiling at him with the tip of her tongue between her teeth.

'And did you stab a man to death?' he struggled to ask; but his tongue denied what his brain demanded.

'The dress . . . the dress you were wearing . . .'

'Oh that! Did you like it, then?'

'Where is it?'

'Don't you fancy this one?'

'The other . . . the – the one you wore before.'

'Do you want me to put it on?'

Martin nodded and the girl, glancing at him curiously, slipped from the room. It was immensely important for him to see her in that dress again. He felt that the sight of it, with all its horrible associations, would give him the strength he needed . . .

'Would you like to buy me a drink, sir?'

She'd come back and was standing before him, swaying slightly and gazing mysteriously down; her eyes were long and shining. She was wearing the dress, the grey and yellow muslin gown. But they were yellow *flowers*, not stars!

He cried out – and put his hand to his eyes. Fiercely he tried to recall the fragment of cloth he'd burned. Stars – stars! They had been yellow stars! He saw them as clearly as if they were before him, blackening in the flame . . .

'What it is?' she whispered uneasily. 'Don't you like me any more?'

He took away his hand and stared wretchedly at the pattern of primroses that swelled over her breast.

'God help me – God help me . . .'

'What is it? What's wrong? Please tell me!'

'Everything . . . no . . . nothing, nothing!'

'Are you – are you laughing – or crying?'

He didn't know. Words, or the sensation of words, rushed through his mind far faster than he could think. Flowers for stars . . . he had burned the stars and been given back flowers . . . a garden full of primroses . . . the primrose way . . .

He felt her hand touch his bowed head. He longed to seize her, to clutch her and bury himself in the yellow flowers –

'If it's me,' she murmured; 'I'm sorry . . . but I thought – you wanted me . . . I wouldn't have . . . with anyone. There's never been . . . But being with you . . . it seemed all right . . . I was so sure . . . Your eyes and smile . . . and the way you made me feel . . . When I said about your gift . . . that was part of it – I'd never have done this otherwise . . . I couldn't help myself . . . It was like there was someone telling, promising . . . Please! If I've done wrong

'... I never knew ... I never meant to – to give offence ...'

'No – no! You haven't ... done wrong! It's you who must forgive!'

'Me? Why?'

Without really meaning to, he knelt before her, and she was frightened. Although she knew nothing, she sensed the upheaval in Martin's heart and soul, and felt helpless in the presence of it.

'Forgive me!' he whispered. 'Please!'

She looked away, and then said suddenly: 'There's someone watching us!'

She went to the window to draw back the curtain; and Martin trembled that not only the curtain, but the girl and the room itself, would gape aside and the giant face of Dr Dormann would be revealed, staring in.

Instead there was nothing but the roots of the iron railings, embedded in the facing brickwork like huge, ungainly stitches.

'There – look!'

Between the railings, like a piece of blown rubbish, caught against the iron, was the inquisitive face of a child.

'Be off with you!'

The child grinned, stuck out its tongue, and vanished.

Chapter Twelve

'An' there they was on the floor – on their knees – like a pair o' cripples doin' a moonlight jig!' recounted Briskitt to Dr Dormann in the stable, after communion – as the nightly drinking of mulberry cordial and the confessions of the sins of others had come to be known.

'And then?'

'They went at it like sparrers – tumblin' an' peckin' an' fumblin' an' –'

'And the gown she put on for him? It was grey and yellow, you say?'

'Grey an' yeller, like I said, Dr Dormann. An' it came orf 'er quick as kiss yer 'and!'

This was Briskitt's invention, and was intended more to please than deceive. He had met with Chops at the bottom of the pit and heard all that his satrap had been able to tell. But it wasn't enough. Briskitt liked to give value for money – even for so little as Dr Dormann's sixpence.

'An' there they was,' said Briskitt dreamily. 'Naked as the day they was born.'

Dr Dormann flashed his teeth and gave Briskitt his sixpence; then he went out through the curtains of the night. A moment later Chops came out of the straw and the two infants gazed at each other with mysterious glee.

Neither really knew what they were about, nor understood the meaning of their employment. They were still too young, and the garden treasured them for that. Mrs Bray was no corrupter of childhood; she would rather have died than have been guilty of spoiling the little ones in her trees. She kept them in her garden only until they reached the time of knowing; and then, like tiny Adams, she cast them out for ever. Generally they were pensioned off to a small apprenticeship in some remote part of the town, where they grew up to useful work and the Mulberry Garden faded from their minds. Briskitt had approached that awesome threshold; he stood in the gateway, half eager, half reluctant, but ultimately, still unknowing . . .

'Go wash your face,' said Briskitt to Chops. 'Can't 'ave our ma ashimed!'

While Chops went out to damp himself in the drinking trough, Briskitt arrayed himself for the coming visit to the lady of his heart. He donned his satin waistcoat, which became him like a Crusader's apron, and assumed two further purchases he had managed to make that night: a cocked hat and a bouquet of roses, red as blood. He stood, stiff and still in the stable, awaiting his squire – a burning knight diminished by a perspective of distance. When Chops returned, admiration robbed him of speech; he gazed upon the splendid Briskitt with religious awe.

'Lead on,' said Briskitt; and knight and squire set out for the castle of the infidel.

They reached the gaol-house as befitted them, in the smallest hours; and the grim gate-keeper let them through with scarcely a nod.

They crossed the moon-washed yard and passed under a low doorway that admitted them to that part of the castle where, in nun-like seclusion, the ladies were lodged.

They mounted the winding stair towards the airy chamber where Chops's ma, in company with six other damsels, was cruelly locked away for the weary space of the night. Upwards and upwards they toiled, with Briskitt's satin waistcoat rising and falling over the pumping of his knees like a brave banner.

At last they reached the chamber of the seven damsels and were admitted by a glowering female gaoler with a key as long as Briskitt's arm. A single taper burned within, in a lantern with bars, so that even the flame was in prison. The dim brown radiance cast by this illuminant lent the room the solemn mystery of a vault in which the seven beds (the gift of a nearby charity) rose and fell and murmured like unquiet tombs.

'Down the end,' whispered Chops; and Briskitt, his heart thundering and his eyes misting, approached 'our ma'.

His shadow crossed her, and the damsel, clad in her knitted shawl, her nearly new shoes and dark stockings as holey as the Pope of Rome, opened her eyes from a drowsiness that was something more than sleep. Dimly she perceived her child – the fruit of her womb – and, in a spasm of sentiment, flung wide her arms, thereby exposing her copious bosom that was scratched from some altercation she couldn't possibly have remembered.

Briskitt gazed down with unfeigned admiration, and, at the same time, felt a pang of anger and distress that an unkind hand should have been laid on her treasures. Silently he offered her the bouquet of roses.

'Oozee?' inquired Chops's ma, becoming aware of the apparition.

'It's Briskitt,' said Chops. 'It's Briskitt come to visit.' Then, turning to his patron, he said with pride: 'It's her. It's our ma.'

'Wassat?' asked the lady, discerning the bouquet.

Briskitt, overcome by the splendour of the occasion, thrust the roses forward until the lady was forced to defend herself by clutching at them. At once she let out a little scream as she pricked herself on the thorns.

The cry awakened her six companions who, with various

106

expressions denoting reproach, rose up and peered towards the cause of the disturbance.

'Flahrs!' said Chops's ma, wonderingly, after she'd sucked her injured fingers and wiped them on her thigh. ''Ee brung me flahrs!'

''Ee brung 'er flahrs!' repeated the damsel opposite, and gazed at the fortunate one who suddenly seemed to be arrayed beyond Solomon in all his glory. 'Flahrs!' went down the sigh, from bed to bed, and deep sniffs sought to catch at the perfume.

'Nick 'em from that there garding?' asked Chops's ma, cautiously inserting her nose among the blooms, which it almost matched, red for red.

Briskitt shook his head.

'He bought 'em!' said Chops, jealous for his patron's reputation. 'He don't nick things for *you*!'

Briskitt nodded and, now having a free hand, reached down, down into the pocket of his waistcoat, and withdrew two gold coins.

'Wassat?' inquired the damsel opposite.

'You mind yer bleedin' business!' said Chops's ma, searching her person feverishly for somewhere to hide the money. 'That there garding looks arter you a treat,' she said eventually, panting from her exertions and making praiseworthy attempts to restore her disarranged modesty.

Briskitt, gazing rapturously at 'our ma's' jampot eyes and billowing bosom, descended into his pocket again. The gift, the keepsake, the talisman with which he was to storm the towers of Jerusalem!

'Wodgergot now?'

Wordlessly he held out the silver locket and chain.

'A-ah!' sighed the damsel opposite. 'Jools!'

Chops's ma, fighting off the miasma of gin that still veiled her sight, struggled upright in her bed. This sudden motion released a great variety of strong odours that caused Briskitt to tremble and feel faint. He swayed backwards –

'Lessavalook!' said Chops's ma, seizing hold of the silver chain before it passed out of reach.

'It's for you,' said Chops, the intermediary.

Bewitched by the bright gift, the damsel studied it by the process of running the chain along her teeth until she came to the obstruction, when she removed the locket from her mouth and fell to examining it with inquisitive care. Suddenly she gave a little cry of startled delight as it sprang open to a lucky touch. Briskitt's eager heart forgot to beat.

'Ugh!' said the lady fastidiously, as the twist of hair fell out. 'Issa worm ora slug or somefing! Issa dirty ol' worm!' She brushed it from her bed with a gesture of revulsion.

'Oh!' A low sound escaped Briskitt, and Chops's ma looked at him.

'Wha' wassit then?' she inquired delicately.

Mutely Briskitt pointed to his head. She stared at the locket, then at the thing she'd brushed to the floor, and back to the long satin waistcoat and the shrunken, quivering face above it.

'Hoo!' she shouted. 'Hoo-hoo-hoo!'

Briskitt looked at Chops in bewilderment and terror. Chops avoided his gaze and stared at his ma. His parent had begun to shake convulsively. She fell back and kicked her legs in the air. She clutched her sides and continued to emit hoot after hoot of helpless female laughter.

'You promised him,' said Chops reproachfully, 'a great big 'ug'nakiss.' He was genuinely alarmed that his mother's behaviour would cost him his patron's friendship and protection.

'Can't stop meself!' she shrieked, and continued to hoot so gustily that she seemed to be blowing Briskitt off his feet. He tottered back . . .

'Shime!' denounced the damsel who'd witnessed the bestowal of gifts. 'You orta took 'im inter bed wiv yer! Lousy stinkin' cow! Shime!'

Briefly Chops's ma peered at her accuser, then her face squashed up again; her jampot eyes vanished and the hooting came on stronger than ever, while her grimy legs thrashed the air.

Briskitt was now half way down the chamber; he tried to put on his hat, but was unable to find his head.

'Shime!' rose up murmurs from the other damsels, who all now joined in heaping reproaches on the head of their ungrateful sister.

'You come over 'ere,' offered a lady, by no means the equal of Chops's ma. Then others added their offers, making strange, bewildering suggestions that buzzed in Briskitt's ears like red hot flies.

He felt something strike him smartly on the back; it turned out to be the door. He banged on it, he kicked it, he tried to bite it – or seemed to do so, for his head was laid against it and his mouth was wide open. At last the glowering female with the key as long as his arm came to set him free.

He ran down the stairs; he ran across the courtyard; he ran without stopping all the way back to the Mulberry Garden. He climbed up into his nest above the twelfth arbour and lay spreadeagled in his kingdom of spiders and leaves.

Blindly he stared down through his spyhole into the darkness below; and Briskitt's face grew dark with rage. The very birds of the air had caught the mocking laughter of Chops's ma.

'I'm done wiv you!' wept Briskitt; and then, including all friends and lovers, all women and the wide world itself in his vast renunciation. 'I'm done wiv the lot of you!'

But pain passes and injury heals; little by little, the mysterious upper garden – the narrow slice of wildness existing between the happy garden and the cold stars – wrapped him up in its minute concerns. He caught a crane-fly and began to remove its legs:

'*Never* no more . . . *never* no more . . . *never* no more . . .'

Chops's ma had lost a generous admirer; but Briskitt had lost far more.

Chapter Thirteen

On the other side of the garden wall stood the other lover, who, having brought no gifts, would seem to have prospered unjustly.

The girl had not committed the crime, and Martin had been spared the agony of pleading with her to confess. The shadowy threat of Dr Dormann had been dispelled, and his gift, the priceless talent without which life, for him, would have lost its grace, had been mysteriously restored.

He felt dazed and elated, as one who had strayed across a battlefield and emerged unscathed. What the forces, what the cause, he knew not. Somehow pity had been taken on him and he had not been required to enlist. His problems now were on a much diminished scale and related only to his feelings for a milliner's girl from Rag Street.

The murder of the apprentice, though it still concerned him professionally, was detached from his heart. It was an alien thing and the evidence he'd burned related to a woman as remote as the stars on her gown.

What was she like, this unknown murderess? He glanced up at the high wall of the Mulberry Garden and wondered uneasily why he had returned there? The sharp glass teeth glinted and seemed about to bite the sky. As he stared and brooded, a girl in stars sauntered through his mind, bearing a knife. Her face was crudely painted, her eyes profound. It was the face of Fanny Bush and, try as he might, he could not strike it out.

The night was airless and quiet. He thought he heard a sound of sobbing coming from the garden. He listened, imagining God knew what: the murderess and the ghost of the youth she'd stabbed . . .

He stood close against the wall, then cursed a slight breeze that sprang up and dissolved the sound he thought he'd heard in the whispering of leaves. The breeze died down, but the sobbing was not renewed; instead another sound had taken its place. It was a sniffing and a tapping, coming closer and closer.

Martin, his mind filled with murder and phantoms and beauty with a knife, turned to look along the street, half expecting to see the woman in stars moving towards him.

But it was a man, tapping his way along the wall by means of a stick. He was accompanied by a black dog, secured to his belt by a length of rope. As they drew near, the dog dragged on the rope and snarled at Martin. It was a hideous, dangerous animal.

'What is it?' asked the blind man. 'Who's there, old girl?'

His face, grey in the starlight, was cobbled with lumps, like the street itself, and he wore a filthy rag round his eyes to advertise his disability.

'Don't you do me no 'arm!' warned the blind man. 'I

ain't got nothing, and if you goes for me, my old bitch will 'ave your throat out!'

'It's all right – it's all right!' said Martin, backing away from the dog. 'I won't harm you! I'm not a thief or a foot-pad ...'

''Course you ain't!' said the blind man, with relief. 'Now I can get a smell of you, I can tell you're a gent. I thought, at first, you was a lady ... but maybe you been somewhere and picked up that pudden pan. That's what must 'ave upset me old girl. Bitches is jealous as knives! Be'ave yourself, old girl!'

He jerked the rope to which the dog was attached and rattled a tin. At once the bitch, as practised a beggar as her master, squatted and gazed up at Martin as if to say: 'I've given him my eyes; what will you give?'

'Spare a coin for me an' me lady,' said the beggar, turning his blind face defencelessly up to the stars.

Martin felt in his pocket and the jingle of coins produced a look of beatific happiness on the blind man's half face.

'You see, old girl? We was both wrong. We come across a good man in the night. It *is* night, ain't it? Generally I tells by the cold; but it's warm now. So I goes by the quiet.'

He held out his tin and deftly opened it with his thumb. Martin put two silver coins among the half dozen or so of copper that the tin contained. Suddenly he started as he saw something else: a pewter medallion with a mulberry tree engraved upon it. He reached to take it out, when the dog growled and snarled warningly.

'That medal you've got in there. Where did you get it?'

'That bit of pewter, sir?'

'Yes ... yes. With the tree on it.'

'So it's a tree, is it? I been puzzlin' about what it might

be. It was give me by a gent in a 'urry. Said it was valuable. Do you want to buy it, sir? I'll trust you to give me a fair price . . .'

'No. I don't want it. When did you get it?'

'Yesterday, I fink. Or it might 'ave been tonight. 'Ee give it me like it was red 'ot. 'Ee were an old gent and smelled it.'

'Did he say anything to you?'

'Oh yes. Very religious gent. Told me I'd been sent by the Lord to take away 'is iniquities into the wilderness. Said 'ee was off 'ome to 'ave a bath an' wash 'is clothes.'

'Did he give you nothing else?'

'No, sir. 'Ee said that the medal 'ad cost 'im plenty.'

Martin sighed deeply, and put two further coins in the scapegoat's tin.

'I wish I could give you more than money, my friend.'

'Money's food an' drink for me and my lady here. What more did you 'ave in mind, sir?'

'Your sight . . . peace, comfort . . .'

'It ain't in your power, sir. I know you means well. But it just ain't in your power. There's limits, you know. Look, sir.'

The blind man, tucking away his tin, turned his face in the direction of Martin's voice and pulled up the filthy bandage. Martin shuddered.

Instead of placidly sunken lids, there were holes in his head, as if his eyes had been torn out by a wild beast. Perhaps it was an illusion of shadows and the night; but before Martin could be sure, the blind man had replaced the bandage.

'I 'as to wear the bandage, else it puts folk off comin' near enough to give me anything. Are you still there, sir?'

'Yes.'

'For a moment I'd a queer feeling you'd run off.'

'Do your . . . eyes give you pain?'

'Sometimes they pricks and aches a bit. They do now.'

Instinctively Martin reached out to touch the bandage; but the dog snarled and made to fly at him.

'I told you, sir, it's not in your power. Even if you could, my old girl here would 'ave your throat out for trying. But there is something you could do, if you 'ad a mind to.'

'What is it?'

'Take me to the Mulberry Garden. I want to go inside it.'

'It's shut. You'll have to wait till it opens tomorrow.'

''Ow much is it to go in? 'Ave I got enough money?'

'That medal you were given. That should take you in.'

'Am I near? I can smell flowers and trees . . .'

'Yes. This is the garden's wall . . .'

'Am I right for the gate?'

'A little further along. But why do you want to go there?'

'There was a young lad killed there, weren't there?'

'Last week . . .'

'And 'ee lost 'is coat.'

'It was never found.'

'Me and my old girl might sniff it out. It's something to look out for. Gives us something to do. Will there be a reward?'

'Perhaps.'

'And could I keep the coat? From all accounts, it ought to be a 'andsome one! I like pretty things, even though I can't see 'em. You 'ear people talk "that's pretty", an' you get an idea in your 'ead like tasting meat and wine. So just point me at the gate, sir, and maybe that medal will bring me and my lady luck.'

Martin did as he was asked, and returned to the vicarage. His mood of elation had left him; the meeting with the blind man had filled him with curious forebodings. The black dog snarling at him, the blind man's rejection of his power and the unexpected sight of the pewter medallion in the tin box all troubled his mind and plagued his sleep till he felt that, far from escaping, he was trapped in the Mulberry Garden more deeply than ever.

At ten o'clock on the Saturday morning Mrs Jackson came to tell him that a gentleman had called to see him urgently. He was waiting in the library. Even before he asked, Martin knew it was Dr Dormann.

Chapter Fourteen

HE stood against the great window, looking like a streak of ink. Strong sunlight flooded all round him so that at first his face was invisible to Martin.

'Good morning – good morning! What a fine one it is! I've never seen such sunshine. The garden can never have too much of it. It drinks the sun!'

Dr Dormann's eager voice betrayed a more noticeable accent than usual; it was almost possible to know his origins. He came across the room and Martin fully expected him to extend a hand to be shaken. He did not know what he would have done in such circumstances; Dr Dormann's hands were large and white and venomously spidery. But no hand was extended.

'I won't keep you long, Mr Young . . . or should I say, "Your Reverence"? I don't care for that title, myself. I noticed your housekeeper refers to you as "master". But I think I'll keep with "Mr Young".'

'What . . . can I do for you, Dr Dormann? I – I am a busy man, you know . . .'

'Yes of course! Up to your eyes in work, I expect! The law of God and the laws of man, eh? My goodness, it must take it out of you! To be honest – if you'll forgive my saying so – you're not looking yourself sir. Your eyes are tired . . . You should rest more. You should enjoy a little of that peace and comfort you try so hard to bring to others! Yes . . . that's my prescription!'

'Are you a doctor of physic?'

'No – no! Not of physic.'

'He's a doctor of nothing!' thought Martin with a rush of bewildered anger. 'I wonder which university?' Not only was he angry, he was also becoming more and more frightened. Despite what was almost a babble of words, delivered in a dryish rustle, it was impossible not to sense a certain poison concealed in them.

Dr Dormann had moved sideways and was now progressing round the walls, fingering the bookshelves as if at random.

'What a fine collection! Some day – if I may – I would like to come and browse. It's so long since I studied! One misses these little luxuries – ah, I see you have the new Concordance! Every word in the Bible! What a task! But the value? Incalculable! Imagine it – one has only to think of, say, taking a random example, "guilt", or "lust", or "charity", and one can go straight to the point at once!'

'Then what *is* it you want with me . . . if you talk of coming to the point?'

'Just a moment! Bear with me, Mr Young. Let me just take out this book and look up "charity". Let's see, for interest, how often it occurs. But what's this? Not once? Ah! How stupid of me! I was looking in the Apocrypha! But it just shows that charity is not apocryphal. It's real. Now here . . . here. Ah! What riches! "*Knowledge puffeth up, but charity edifieth.*" True, true! "*But the greatest of these is charity.*" Again, how true! And here it says: "*For charity shall cover sins.*"'

His finger lingered on the place, then he snapped the book shut and returned it to the shelf.

'I deceived you, Mr Young. The words I chose were not entirely at random. It's charity I've really come for,' he said, and a shaft of hatred seemed to shine out of the man like a beam from a black sun.

'What do you mean . . . charity?'

'Ah! There's a girl, you see. Very poor; but that's not it. Poverty's no sin, and, as it says, charity shall cover *sins*.

That's the nub of it! I'm sorry – so sorry! I didn't mean to use that ugly word! *Nub*. I intended "heart", but, of course, nub has another meaning. Hang. Hang by the neck until dead.

'But let's put hanging out of our minds and go back to the girl. Would you believe it, she did a foolish thing! Imagine this: she stabbed a man. Yes, stabbed him in the heart and he languished and died, as they say at inquests and places where they inquire.'

'She didn't! She didn't!' cried Martin, suddenly triumphant.

'There speaks the generous man, eager to protect! There speaks the man who would do anything rather than see the young girl hanged by the neck! And he did, you know; do anything, I mean. Oh yes. You may not credit this, but I assure you it is so. He actually took away and hid from everyone a fragment of that girl's dress that would certainly have damned her. And what do you think he did then? Why he burned it. He actually burned it in a church! What a thing to do for love. I'm sure it was love, not lust ... although he claimed his reward in the girl's room. But it was love. They both knelt ...'

Martin was trembling violently. How was it possible for the devil to have known all this?

'So now you can see, Mr Young, that the cause is a worthy one. The charity I ask is for both of them. I assure you, it will cover both of them. A hundred pounds. A trifle really. But much needed in the circumstances, and, as they say, it's the thought that counts. And if you'll pardon me for wrenching the conversation a little; remember: "*Knowledge puffeth up, but charity edifieth.*" In other words, now you know, now you give. And in exchange, sir, allow me to offer you this.'

He had fumbled in his coat pocket and withdrawn his

sheet of a hand. In it lay a pewter medallion with the design of a mulberry tree.

'A token, sir. A token. Nothing more. And yet, a pledge of faith on both sides. Possess it and come to the garden when you will. Absolutely no extra charge. Enjoy the freedom, enjoy the company . . . Upon my word of honour, Mr Young, you'll never regret it!'

'But you're wrong, you're wrong. She didn't do it! The cloth was not the same! She wore flowers – the other was stars! I told you you were wrong! There's nothing you can do! Get out of here, you madman!'

For a moment Dr Dormann looked indeed somewhat taken aback. He grew, if possible, even whiter and seemed to be affected by a chill. Then he recovered himself.

'Stars, you say? Are you sure? The feeble light and memory can play tricks. Stars, after all, are the flowers of the sky. I think they were flowers. But what does it matter now? The fragment is destroyed. Nothing remains but a memory of stars and a reality of flowers. I like the imagery; but I see that it troubles you, sir. Are you beginning to doubt your memory? Is it not possible that they *were* flowers? But it doesn't matter in the end. You burned the cloth and, with it, that poor girl's innocence. That's irony; that's tragedy, Mr Young. Surely that's the sin that charity must cover. Give me the hundred pounds and take the medallion, and then I'll go, sir. I know you are busy and there's the morning service waiting . . .'

The man had somehow drifted very close to Martin. He had the indistinct impression that he had been propelled rather than moved of his own volition. His protruding eyes seemed to have independent fires in them which totally belied the nervous, ineffectual twisting of his mouth into various semblances of smiles. This was a man who was surely possessed by the devil . . .

'No...no...no!' cried Martin, backing away as a feeling of obscenity came out of the man like a thick vapour. He had a frantic and wholly stupid idea of flinging a crucifix at him – of hurling him down a mountain side –

'I beg of you,' said Dr Dormann, staring towards the door and manifesting obvious signs of uneasiness and concern at the fury he'd awakened, 'don't, please don't decide now, Mr Young! There is time ... until Friday. We live from Friday to Friday ... and we die on Fridays, too. Why did I say that?'

'Get out – get out!'

'Oh I'll go, sir. I'm going. But it will do no good. You cannot hide. You are watched, you know. Do you remember the Lesson? "*And a watcher came down?*" There is no escape ... there is no – ah!'

Martin, in the extremity of his desperation and revulsion from Dr Dormann, had seized a heavy book and flung it at him. The volume caught the doctor on the side of the head. He staggered and half fell to the ground. Instinctively Martin went forward to see if the man was really injured.

Dr Dormann raised his hand as if to defend himself from a second attack. He was almost grey in the face and was trembling so that his ill-fitting teeth threatened to jump out. He worked his lips over them urgently.

'I'm sorry,' muttered Martin, much ashamed. 'I didn't mean to –'

'No...no! That – that is not necessary. I – I – You must excuse me ... I – I am unwell. I should have told you ... I am a sufferer. A moment, Mr Young. Let me ... recover myself. Perhaps, if it's not asking too much ... your housekeeper might let – let me have a glass of water? Outside, of course, if you want. I will go ... yes, I will go;

but I must sit down first. In the hall ... anywhere. It is a condition, you know ... I cannot stop it ...'

Even as Martin bent over him, the skin on his face seemed to come up in a curious, colourless rash – like roughened paper. It was almost as if he had something pasted over his whole face.

He stayed about half an hour, after being helped down to the little whitewashed room by the kitchen. There were two other callers waiting, who watched him with embarrassment and sympathy. When he had recovered, they shook him by the hand and declared that he could not have done better than to call upon the saintly Mr Young.

Chapter Fifteen

DR DORMANN made his way, in a dazed and sick condition, towards Cuper's Pyrotechnic Factory of Turnmill Street. He had by no means recovered from his appalling and embarrassing seizure, which was one of the worst he had ever had; but the need to escape from the vicarage overcame his physical weakness.

He was aware that passers-by looked at him with concern, but he could not bear the thought of assistance or of anyone talking to him, so he stopped for several minutes in a public house and took a glass of brandy. He sat in a corner, looking as corpselike as if he'd been carved out of a wax candle. The publican did not like the look of him at all, but Dr Dormann's clerical appearance gained him a certain amount of respect.

He had no particular thoughts in his mind; he felt quite drained of everything. The forces that governed him would seem to have abandoned him, leaving behind a shell that was peculiarly uncomfortable to inhabit.

He finished his brandy and the publican inquired if he would take another? Dr Dormann gave a frightful smile and shook his head; he rarely drank spirits, and then only in the strictest moderation. He left the public house and continued on his way to Turnmill Street, to arrange with Mr Cuper about Mrs Bray's fireworks.

He was certainly feeling better now; perhaps it was the brandy, or the thought of bringing off some shrewd stroke of business to oblige his mistress. He really was the most devoted of servants . . .

Cuper's Factory was in a narrow lane known as Frying-Pan Alley. Originally it was said to have been Firing-Pan

Alley, as a gun-maker was reputed to have lived there, and Mr Cuper had once tried to revive the earlier, more suitable name, by having it printed on his trade card. But, as no one had ever heard of Firing-Pan Alley, he gave up and went from the fire back to the frying-pan. Either way, it smelled of explosions and burning. It was hard to say *what* had been burning; it might have been paper, wood, salt-petre, apprentices, or a mixture of them all.

The Factory, dull, low and battered outside, was tre-mendous within, owing to sundry small fires that, over the passage of years, had destroyed all the inner partitions and doors, leaving only blackened frames on which the apprentices and journeymen hung their coats.

Illumination in this cavernous place – which resembled a war-torn town – was provided by candles enclosed in long glass funnels – one to each workman. From time to time, one or other of these candles would spring into an eye-searing brilliance as a journeyman would test the powder he was preparing by sprinkling it into the flame. Bouquets of stars would erupt and remain imprinted on the inner eye for seconds after they had died. The general effect of coming into this place, with its ceaseless explosions of sparkling fire and the dark, demonic figures of the experimenting journeymen, was that one had strayed into the bowels of creation and witnessed apprentice gods try-ing their hands at universes.

Mr Cuper came forward to greet Dr Dormann. The master-pyrotechnician was a serious, grey-haired man wanting an eye – though from the brightness of the one that remained he didn't really want the other for more than ornament.

'I want to arrange for a display,' said Dr Dormann, flinching a little as the stars blazed and spat, and seemed to threaten all with instant ruin.

'Wedding, birthday, confinement – or political?' Mr Cuper's solitary eye, far from shrinking, seemed to leap out of its socket with each silent explosion.

'For the Mulberry Garden.'

'I know it. Clerkenwell. Mrs Bray.'

'We would like it on a Friday night . . .'

'Saturday's better,' said Mr Cuper, with a craftsman's authority. 'More of a crowd.'

'Mrs Bray particularly asked for Friday,' said Dr Dormann, staring up at the black ceiling where a violent constellation had just gone out.

'Friday it is!' said Mr Cuper. 'That's enough there!'

This latter was to an apprentice who was attempting to ignite a mound of powder he had scraped together on his bench.

'They're like children, you know. No notion of the cosmic consequences. Put an army of children in the field and they'd destroy more than Attila and all his Huns! But one mustn't be too hard. Innocence always plays with fire. It takes experience to know that fire is warmth, light and beauty. It takes experience to see the cosmic in it. I used to put something of that kind on my trade card; but the printer put it in Latin and nobody knew what it meant. So you must have a Friday?'

He turned up an almanack that hung on a string from a nail in a charred door frame.

'The sixth of September,' he said, fixing the day with a worn and blistered finger.

'Could it not be before?'

'It's the moon. There's no moon on the sixth. You'd be amazed at the harm a moon can do. There's absolutely no competing with it. Set-pieces costing hundreds can sometimes go for nothing when there's a moon about. Now, sir – what is it that you have in mind? Something ambitious,

I hope? A scene, perhaps? St George and the Dragon? Or what about the burning of Sodom and Gomorrah? No; on second thoughts that's hardly the thing for a pleasure garden, eh? How much are you prepared to spend?'

'Mrs Bray mentioned twenty pounds.'

'So large a lady and so small a sum?' Mr Cuper looked surprised. His eyes widened reproachfully. 'I'm afraid twenty pounds will yield you very little. Twenty pounds might suffice for a private house and the birth of a second son; but for a pleasure garden? I'm afraid I can do nothing for you, sir, that would not bring discredit on us both.'

'How much more would you need, Mr Cuper . . . to do us both credit?'

'Ah! Let me show you.' Mr Cuper clapped his hands and the journeymen desisted from their star-making. He led Dr Dormann from bench to bench and showed him the patterns of the pieces that were being manufactured.

'Here is a grotto with a serpent breathing fire; cost, seventy-five pounds. Here is Moses and the burning bush; cost, sixty pounds. Here is Elijah in his burning fiery chariot; cost, sixty-five pounds. Here are the Children of Israel led at night by a pillar of fire; cost, a hundred pounds. Costly but cosmic, my dear sir. All the pieces are, of course, erected by us upon stout cane and bound with wire and include an overture of rockets, serpents and saucissons . . .'

As each journeyman and apprentice displayed his work, Dr Dormann observed the nightmarish fact that there was not a whole person among them. One man lacked two fingers, another had lost his thumb; an apprentice had a great hole in the top of his ear, while another had lost that member altogether and had nothing but a labyrinth in the side of his head. The last to show was a lad in his third year who had neither lashes nor eyebrows and only half a nose.

'There must be no bangs,' said Dr Dormann, remembering the care his mistress had laid upon him. 'Nothing to frighten . . .'

'Reports, sir; we call them reports. It is the saucissons that are reported. They can, of course, be omitted, or you may have them unreported. I assure you, the effect of noiseless explosions, with a quantity of greenish or reddish smoke, can be quite cosmic.'

'That piece over there,' said Dr Dormann suddenly. 'How much would it cost?'

Mr Cuper looked round, and, observing a vast, unwieldy structure leaning against a wall, smiled appreciatively.

'I think you may be fortunate there. I'd forgotten it. It is a piece that was made up for a theatrical performance that unfortunately went bankrupt. You could have that quite reasonably. Including the cost of erection, supervision of fuses, et cetera, et cetera, I could do it for, say, fifty-five pounds.'

'It is of masks, isn't it?'

'Comedy and Tragedy with a scroll of serpents. You will observe the wheels in the mouths of the snakes? When ignited, they revolve and discharge red smoke. The effect is quite cosmic, I can promise you. There is also an additional effect that I invented myself. I won't tell you what it is as it has to be seen to be believed. Cosmic is the only word for it.'

'I suppose this Friday is out of the question? There is a masquerade in the garden and it would have been very apt.'

'Out of the question, sir.'

'Then, if I decide, will it be ready for the following Friday?'

'We will move heaven and earth to oblige you, sir.

Heaven and earth. But there is one thing of which I must warn you. You will find it plainly put on my trade card. We cannot, under any circumstances, be held responsible for the effects of rain. I have known a spring shower quite put out Nebuchadnezzar's burning fiery furnace!'

Dr Dormann returned to the Mulberry Garden. He had spent thirty-five pounds of his own money and would have cut out his tongue rather than admit it to Mrs Bray who would not have thanked him for his extravagance. The reek and flash of the factory, with its eyeless, earless, fingerless workers lingered in his mind and gave him a meditative air which Mrs Bray was quick to pounce upon.

'You've paid a call, Dr D. You've paid one of your Saturday calls. I can always tell. It's your eyes. They puff up and go bloodshot – as if you'd had a night on the tiles. It didn't go well, did it? You'd have been smiling and all over me otherwise. Well – well! Don't take it so hard!' She laughed good-naturedly. 'Who was it showed you the door? Or was it his boot, this time?'

'It was . . . Martin Young,' muttered Dr Dormann, utterly unable to lie or even to conceal anything from the enormous woman.

The smile left her countenance, and a vein in the region of her neck began to throb and struggle.

'Why, you stupid little man,' she began quietly. 'I warned you about that one. You knew I dreamed of blood on his page. Why did you do it? Why did you go against me?'

She paused, but not for an answer; she knew quite well that none could be forthcoming. She paused, rather, in the way a great wave might seem to pause, trembling only a little at its crest, before it falls with a roar like thunder and smashes even rocks into fragments.

She began to shout, to scream at him. She called him every foul and filthy name she could lay tongue to; she cursed every part of him, sparing nothing – nothing! She cursed the day that had given him birth, and the woman who had brought forth such a reptile. She cursed the day that ever she had seen him – and prayed for the day that would be his last.

The very parlour in which she sat trembled and shook with her gigantic fury, till it seemed that the walls must split and the air be rent in two. Dr Dormann clapped his hands to his ears, but he could no more shut out the woman's rage than he could have halted an earthquake; so he covered his face and his spidery fingers writhed as if they would tear away the skin beneath.

At last the chief of her fury was spent and the room lapsed into shaken quiet, broken only by her profound breathing.

'And you failed,' she said, moderating her voice but with pitiless anger. 'That's the worst of it. What if he strikes back? I'll tell you what. You're on your own, my friend. I want to know nothing about it. Nothing, I tell you. Don't you dare breathe a word to me of what's gone on! The guilt is all yours. If anybody's going to suffer, it will be you, my friend. You'll be the one who goes . . . to hell, for all I care!'

Dr Dormann lowered his hands; long, livid marks covered his face. Mrs Bray stared at him long and hard; and then, quite suddenly, she began to smile and chuckle with an enormous gaiety, as if all the time it had been bubbling away under her wrath and had at last broken through.

'What a sight! There's no call to look so down in the mouth! You just finish what you've begun. Who knows? You may bring it off! It's either him or you. And I'll tell you what, you poor little man —' She broke off to laugh till she shook with a creaking as of great branches, heavily laden. 'Tell you what! You just bring Mr Young in with one of our medals on his heart and — and I'll give you a great big hug and a kiss and say no more about it! There, now! I know you meant well, so I'll say, God bless you, Dr. D. . . .'

Dr Dormann left the parlour with a sense of almost hysterical relief . . . as of a man whose life has been suddenly and inexplicably spared. Had she raised a weapon to him — an axe — he would have been powerless to stop her smashing it down on his head. He knew it and trembled at the thought. But, instead, she had chosen to laugh as if all the time she really understood, or divined, the terrific pressure within him that had forced him to act against her wishes. Or perhaps they *had* been her wishes but for some reason of her own she wanted to hide them from him and make it seem that he was acting independently?

But — and he knew this was a dreadful conviction — even though she understood him, if he failed she would cast him out. She would throw him away like a burned-out faggot.

Almost mechanically he walked towards the stable to see if the watcher he had set on his enemy had returned. An uneasiness had overcast his thoughts. In such a state as he was in, the spectre of failure was peculiarly strong; and everything contributed to it so that he knew no peace.

The discovery that the girl from Rag Street was almost certainly innocent of the crime (he had believed Martin in that), had been a real blow. It had shaken him considerably; and it was only when his inner daemon had persuaded him that it was really for the best — that the man, Martin Young, was more likely to fall in attempting to protect the innocent than the guilty — that his energies returned. Of course it was true! The man would never have compromised himself, when it came to it, to shield a murderess. But to protect someone *he himself* had placed in danger by his own blind folly? He would come, cap in hand, to the garden. That was certain.

But what if he should find the other, the woman in stars – the murderess herself – between now and the day appointed? Then everything would be lost. What if, at this very minute, his enemy was searching, inquiring and drawing near to the murderess? His uneasiness increased and his daemon whispered: 'You must find her first!'

He reached the stable door and stared inside. A child rose up out of the straw with the look of guilt every child greeted him with. It was not the watcher but his companion.

'My ma's poorly,' said Chops defensively, as if illness excused everything.

Dr Dormann nodded. 'Where is your friend?'

'Briskitt won't come and see her,' said Chops, by way of an answer, and stared down meaningly at Briskitt's model ship, which he had found and removed from its hiding-place to contemplate with aching envy.

'That's a fine vessel . . .'

'Briskitt bought it. He's rich. Rich as old Nick and he won't come and see my ma.'

'How is Briskitt so rich? Does he steal? Stealing is wicked and thieves go to hell.'

'That's where Briskitt told me to tell my ma to go. Hell. He's hard as nails since he got rich.'

'Where does he get all his money?'

'Dunno. You'd best ask him yourself, Dr Dormann, sir,' said Chops, suddenly alarmed by his betrayal. 'He's coming now!'

Chapter Sixteen

THE woman in stars! She haunted Martin; she was continually in his mind and even in the corner of his eye. He saw her a thousand times in the course of a single day, flickering round corners, vanishing among street crowds, disappearing into shops . . . On the Sunday he saw her in the congregation and stumbled haplessly during the responses. Afterwards he stood in the porch and stared and stared into the throng coming out of the church; but she was not there.

The really horrible thing about it was that her face was always the painted mask that Fanny Bush had worn when she'd tried to be a whore. The unknown murderess taunted him and ceaselessly reminded him of his criminal folly and how easily he'd been tripped so that his heels kicked at heaven.

Mrs Jackson was deeply concerned for him; although her mind was primitive in its simple faith and superstition, her instincts were sharp and her love and veneration for Martin were boundless. She sensed that Martin was not so much ill as in some crisis of spirit; accordingly she took every opportunity of recollecting those tales she'd regaled him with in childhood of brawny Scottish saints (canonized in her mind alone) who'd cast down the devil in strenuous contests from Gretna Green to the Isle of Mull.

'And how did they know him?' asked Martin, smiling wearily. 'Were they lucky enough to spot the cloven hoof?'

'Dinna you mock, master. Ye know as well as any that the de'il may come in all forms and fashions . . . sometimes as a fine gentleman, sometimes as a great leddy. He appeared to St Joseph of Pitlochry as an angel; but guid St Joseph knew him and cast him down into the Garry. 'Tis the quality of a saint, master, that he knows the de'il for what he is.'

She gazed at him with a wonderfully penetrating look of love and awe.

'If ye was to meet with the de'il, master, ye'd know him. There's nae a doubt of it!'

'And would I be able to cast him down?'

'E'en if he offered ye the wurrld for your shoe-buckle, ye'd cast him down, master!'

On the Monday he went to Rag Street. Although he longed to, he did not go to see Fanny. He felt guilty and frightened on account of the danger in which she unknowingly stood. Her innocence of everything was a cross he was unequal to bearing; and the undoubted fact that his gift had been turned against her and himself produced in him a sense of distress and shame from which there seemed no relief.

He went to Rag Street to search the shops and stalls in the frail hope that the murderess might have ridded herself there of the incriminating gown. He peered through filthy glass at mountains of discarded garments and marvelled that anyone could have worn them so long . . . and then supposed them still of use to others. Nothing seemed too far gone but that someone might have need of it.

He dragged his way through reeking bundles, stacked on pavement stalls: dresses that had once been a pride and joy; that had been danced in, kissed in, admired in, made love in, married in, and maybe even died in; but where was the dress a woman had murdered in?

He went inside the shops, inquiring for a muslin gown,

cunningly saying that he wanted it for a poor parishioner who had set her heart on such a thing. His charity was applauded and no one grew sharp when, for one reason or another, nothing turned out to be quite what he had in mind. There never was a gown with yellow stars on a grey sky.

At times, during this hopeless quest, he had the strange sensation that he was following in someone else's footsteps; but this might well have been because, in his distraction of mind, he visited some shops twice.

Then it occurred to him to inquire about coats. The profusion of clothing, and the constant elbowing past of those with limp garments to sell, recalled to him the jury-man's opinion at the inquest that the murdered youth's coat had been carried away for the purpose of selling it.

But here he was going over old ground; such inquiries had already been made without success. Besides, there had always been uncertainty as to what the youth had been wearing on the night he'd been killed. His employer had been vague and his friends had not been familiar with the extent of his wardrobe. The blind beggar and his dog – the battered scapegoat Martin had met on the Friday night – was more likely than he to find the vanished coat.

Yet – and here was the maddening part – any of the disembodied coats that lurked in shadows or posed legless in the murky air might have been the very one, and the shopkeeper, taxed with it, might have been able to say who brought it in . . . ('Yes, yes! I remember! It was a woman in yellow stars. I know her well . . .')

He left Rag Street feeling more and more that he was pursuing a dream. He felt that the end of the affair already existed – and that it was disaster, and he was merely reliving certain days of a path down which he'd already trod, wrongly believing it to be hopeful.

He went to Goswell Street to call upon the staymaker who had employed Isaac Fisk. It was possible that the man, or one of his family, had by now remembered something, perhaps had discovered that a coat known to have been in Fisk's possession was no longer among his possessions.

The master staymaker, whose name, in accordance with an ancient custom, was Wishbone, greeted Martin courteously, and then, with a curious mixture of secrecy and respect, invited him to step within.

Strange perfumes filled the air, as if incense had been burned, and there was a cushioned quiet that descended when the door was closed. Martin followed the staymaker through a good-sized parlour or showroom, where a painting of a mythological subject hung upon the wall, and into a private office.

'How can I help you, Mr Young?' he asked gently, and gestured towards a chair.

Mr Wishbone was a slight, mournful-looking man with immensely strong hands, deeply scored from the exercise of his mysterious craft.

'I wondered,' said Martin, seating himself, 'if you or any of your family have remembered anything about the coat your apprentice might have been wearing on the night that – that he was killed?'

The staymaker sighed and shook his head.

'As I told the coroner, sir, poor Isaac had more coats than one, you know. He was fond of clothes – God rest his soul! He was forever picking up oddments in Rag Street. One never knew, from one day to another, what he'd appear in. He was like a child – always drawn to the bright and gaudy ...'

'Is it possible that a servant might have noticed . . . or even one of your family? A daughter, perhaps?'

The staymaker compressed his lips slightly and seated himself at a desk on which there lay several strips of whale-fin and lengths of stout canvas.

'I can assure you, sir, that my daughter would have paid no attention to the comings and goings of Isaac Fisk – may he rest in peace!'

He picked up a strip of whale-fin and, under the stress of some disturbing recollection, bent it and twisted it, gazing at the resulting shapes with profound dissatisfaction.

'I thought – I understood that he was a well-enough-liked young fellow? There was nothing that anyone said that suggested –'

'– Oh yes, yes!' interrupted the staymaker, hurriedly. 'He was, as you say, well enough liked.'

'You seem doubtful, Mr Wishbone. Is there anyone you know of who might have had reason to –'

'– No, no!' interrupted the staymaker again and, at the same time, released the whale-fin so that it snapped straight and quivered upright like a warning finger. 'There was nothing like that, sir. I don't want to speak ill of the dead, you understand; but it was just that he was a little – *young*. I think that's the best one can say. Perhaps it was our craft that confused him? Who can tell now? If you asked me, I would say that he lacked – he lacked –' The staymaker looked round as if the word he sought was somewhere in the air; 'reverence', he came out with finally.

'This is a craft, sir, that requires *reverence*.' He lowered his voice, and the general air of secrecy in the little office closed in like an invisible hand. 'We approach, you know, very close to the sex. It is a trust, sir; a sacred trust. We see; we measure; we touch; we shape. We know more than the lover, more than the husband. We know ... *everything*, sir. But we must have reverence. The ladies, sir, are goddesses; and they must have their mysteries.'

'And this apprentice of yours?'

The master staymaker closed his eyes and sighed with ineffable sadness.

'He was, how shall I put it? – he was *eager*, sir. I blame myself for not having understood. The trade was too much for him. He hadn't that sense of vocation. To be so close, and yet be reverent, was simply not in him. It was his nature, you see. I am not exaggerating, sir, when I say that the mysteries *affected* him. He was woman-mad.' Mr Wishbone's voice sank to the merest thread of a whisper. 'I dared not let him near the younger ones. He – he never touched, you understand; he *felt*.'

He uttered the last word as if repeating a vile blasphemy. He sighed again, shook his head and stood up.

'This is, of course, confidential, sir. There is no point in casting stones at the dead. But as you are here, perhaps you would like to examine his possessions for yourself and maybe form some idea of the garment that was lost?'

Martin nodded and Mr Wishbone conducted him downstairs to his workroom where the apprentices lived and the deeper mysteries were practised.

The room was large and bright with jigging candles; hoops, stays, stomachers and those bony cases for infirm breasts called 'jumps' stood stock still round the walls and in the corners, like love's skeletons, waiting an invitation to the dance. Trim waists, proud hips and amorous bosoms leafed through the mind in this uncanny place, where phantom fragments of women awaited the immortal breath of life.

Mr Wishbone stood for a moment, lost in melancholy admiration, when among the wire and bones, something stirred. A young apprentice, with the face of an angel seen in a cage, concealed something guiltily under a piece of canvas.

Pricked by curiosity, Martin approached the bench and, despite the angel's look of mute dismay, lifted the canvas – and discreetly lowered it again.

The apprentice gazed gratefully at Martin; and Martin shook his head reproachfully, but could not contain a smile. The object under the canvas had been a longbow, fashioned out of the flexible materials of the trade. But where was the arrow? Martin glanced round the room to see who had been shot to the heart. She was not hard to find. Against a wall stood half a bony lady, struck down before her prime by a whale-fin arrow with a canvas flight.

'Surely,' said Martin, picking up a pair of stays to distract the master and give the guilty archer a chance to recover his weapon unobserved, 'no waist can be as small as this?'

'My dear Mr Young,' said the staymaker, smiling with mournful pride, 'you really must not question the shapes it is our duty and privilege to give the ladies.'

He took the stays from Martin and held them reverently in his powerful hands, while the apprentice, with another grateful look at Martin, went to recover his telltale arrow.

'The shapes, sir,' mused Mr Wishbone, 'are not of our deciding. In the deepest sense, they suggest themselves. That is to say, each lady declares herself to the craftsman without so much as uttering a single word. She has no need to. One senses, sir, how best a lady's spirit or personage should be presented. One goes by the lips, the mouth. Now you, being a clergyman, might well ask, why not the eyes? Are not the eyes the windows of the soul? That is undoubtedly so with gentlemen. But the ladies do not have what you and I understand by souls. They are different. They are goddesses and their inmost nature is in their lips, their mouths ... What are you doing there, boy?'

'Nothing, Mr Wishbone, sir,' said the apprentice, who, having unbalanced his late target while removing the arrow, was endeavouring to restore it. 'Just straightening, sir.'

Mr Wishbone stared at the skeleton shape in a distracted fashion.

'Have you come across it yet? You know what I mean ...'

'No, sir. I've not found it.'

Mr Wishbone shook his head, and then, recollecting the object of Martin's visit, went to draw aside a curtain that concealed a shallow alcove.

'Here are poor Isaac's belongings. His family will be collecting them soon, I'm told. I hope so ... I hope so. I don't like keeping them here ... in this room.'

Martin looked on the sad remains of Isaac Fisk. Two pairs of breeches and some items of linen were neatly folded on a shelf, and above, from hooks in the wall, hung three bright coats, like sleeping butterflies.

'You can see what I mean,' murmured Mr Wishbone; and Martin involuntarily reached forward and touched the coats as if the ghost of Isaac Fisk was in one of the pockets, only waiting to be freed and shriek for vengeance.

'The other coat was bound to be ... the same. What is it now?'

The apprentice had approached and was standing beside Martin with a general air of helpfulness.

'What is it you want?'

'If you please, sir, I think all his coats are here.'

'What makes you say that?' asked Martin, with a sudden chill of excitement.

'He doesn't know,' interposed Mr Wishbone peevishly. 'He's only started this week. He never even laid eyes on Isaac Fisk.'

'Is that true?'

The apprentice nodded, but was undeterred. His sense of gratitude to Martin transcended his awe of his master.

'I never saw him, sir; but I looked over his things.'

'And what did you learn from them?'

'Only that he looked after them proper. If he'd had another coat he'd have put up another hook for it. Now as there ain't no empty hooks, sir, there weren't another coat.'

'He would hardly have needed a hook for the coat he was wearing,' said Mr Wishbone in a voice that plainly warned the new apprentice to refrain from exercising his ingenuity at his master's expense.

'No, sir. I hadn't thought of that. But what about when he got undressed for bed? Wouldn't he have needed to hang it up then?'

'Better brains than yours, my boy, have decided that there *was* another coat. So let's hear no more from you, eh? If you must exercise your wits, set about finding that dress that's disappeared.'

'Dress?' said Martin sharply. 'What dress? Have you lost a gown, then?'

'Not a customer's, I assure you!' said Mr Wishbone hastily. 'It was nothing ... only an old gown of my wife's. It used to hang there –' (he pointed to the apprentice's target). 'It was useful, you understand ... to get an idea ... But as a garment, it was worthless. Scarcely fit for Rag Street. But nevertheless, it served to cover ... to give a sense, so to speak.'

'What was it like . . . this missing gown?'

'Like all Mrs Wishbone's clothes. It was in good taste. It was a summery gown. In muslin. Yes. It was grey muslin with a pattern of yellow stars . . .'

Chapter Seventeen

So he had found her at last – the woman in the grey muslin dress patterned with stars! As in a storm when a flash of lightning throws up God knows what monsters as trees, clear and black in every fleeting detail, so the crime presented, for an instant, its true face.

The coat that was not missing, and the gown that was, transposed themselves in Martin's mind; he saw with meticulous clarity that Isaac Fisk had taken the gown, had gone into the garden wearing it, had been stabbed in it and had clutched at a fragment as it had been torn away from his dying hand.

Martin left Goswell Street shaken and bewildered by the discovery. As he walked back, it seemed to him that the phantom he had been pursuing earlier, far from vanishing or remaining in the corner of his eye, now swayed and hovered in front of him, smiling maliciously with the pretty, spiteful face of Isaac Fisk. He could not rid himself of this chimera, nor of the frightening, uncanny sensations it awoke in him. The streets tilted and swam away as the youth in stars jigged and hopped and put out his tongue, which was sometimes forked and sometimes bright as a knife.

The crowds pushed and buffeted him, so that he began to lose all sense of place and direction. Once he stumbled over a projecting cellar step and fell heavily. A child, whose face looked vaguely familiar (all children looked alike), helped him to his feet and, dazed from his fall, he rewarded the child with a guinea. The child stared at him with incredulous gratitude – and vanished as if into a hole in the air.

At last he reached his house and shut himself away in the library, but the phantom would not leave him alone; it continually parted his thoughts and interposed itself everywhere, even among the multitudinous concerns of his daily life.

'What were you, Isaac Fisk?' he whispered.

'Don't you know?' countered the equivocal phantom, smiling with secret eyes. 'I was young; I was eager; I was ... inquisitive.'

'What was in your mind when you put on that gown? Who was it you were going to meet with?'

'A man ... a woman ... a girl ... Like my master said, the trade confused me. So near the sex, you understand. Measuring, touching, *feeling*. Feeling's a sin ... he-he!' (The phantom chuckled and widened its girlish eyes.) 'I was a man ...'

'You were ... young.'

'I was young. I was a man ... I was a woman ... I had a woman's mouth ... and a man's eyes. I was both ... I was neither ...'

'Who killed you, Isaac Fisk? Was it because of that crime against nature?'

'Murder's the only crime against nature. And I was murdered ...'

'Then why – why?'

'Yes! That's it! Why – why – why!'

Helplessly Martin found himself enmeshed in this eerie and insubstantial dialogue, that seemed to be taking place in the night-time of the spirit, and always returned to the same question: why – why?

At last Mrs Jackson could no longer refrain from interrupting him. She came into the library, flushed and apologetic.

'What is it, Mrs Jackson?'

'I've already sent many a puir body away, master; but

143

there's someone come fra the gaol-house who'll no take no for an answer.'

'What do they want with me?'

'It's one o' the puir wummin. She's been took grievous bad. She's on her deathbed, the puir thing, and it's time for the priest, they say.'

'Then send for the curate. He can read a prayer as well as I can.'

'Oh master! Ye know quite well that that one couldna bring comfort to a silk cushion! Sinner that the wumman may be, she's a right to your gift.'

'Oh yes, my gift,' said Martin bitterly; and prepared to leave the vicarage for Bridewell Gaol.

The governor – a small, fat, greasy man whose life was overshadowed by the constant fear that his guilty charges were plotting behind his back – greeted Martin at the entrance to the women's quarters.

'It's not my fault, your reverence. I do everything I can –'

'No one's blaming you. Is she – still alive?'

'Oh yes, yes! Or at least, she was a half-hour ago.'

'Is it a fever?'

'Gin – gin! She's poisoned herself with the damned stuff! I don't know where they get it. I do everything I can . . . but I think there's some sort of conspiracy . . . in fact, I'm sure of it! Will there be an inquiry?'

'Let's hope she recovers.'

'Oh she'll die all right!' muttered the governor, in a tone that implied pretty plainly that it would be done only to spite him.

He beckoned to Martin and began to mount the winding stair.

'Is there any family?'

'No. Oh yes – yes. There's a child, I'm told. A male child; a mere scrap of humanity. Something else to be cleared up, I suppose.'

The governor's shoulders hunched defensively as if this, too, was a part of the all-pervasive plot against him.

'Has she a husband?'

'A husband? That would be a luxury for Mogg! That's her name, you know: Mogg!'

At last he arrived panting at the topmost stair, where a female turnkey was waiting.

'She's sleeping now, your honour.'

The governor heaved a sigh of relief and hurried back down the stairs, anxious to escape before the woman Mogg could strike her final blow at him by dying in his presence.

'She's the one down the end,' said the turnkey, and admitted Martin to the chamber of the seven damsels.

Chops's ma lay on her bed with her eyes closed but everything else about her wide open: her mouth, her loose bosom and her grimy, half-stockinged legs.

The turnkey dragged in a chair and Martin sat down and opened the book of Common Prayer. As he waited for the woman to show some signs of comprehension, one of the other prisoners slopped down the room and, pushing past him, drew a covering over Chops's ma's shameless legs. (They are goddesses, thought Martin; and must have their mysteries.)

He smiled gratefully at this other woman, who nodded and remained standing by the bed. She gestured to the place opposite, indicating that she was a close neighbour and the nearest thing to a friend that the woman Mogg had ever had.

'Her child?' murmured Martin. 'Where is he?'

'Comes in late of a night. Works in the Mulberry Garding.'

Martin frowned slightly as the uncanny pleasure garden intruded itself. The woman, catching his expression, added:

'He ain't the only one. Lots of 'em work there ... an' get looked arter. They'll care for 'im all right.'

He bowed his head as the garden, like the crime, presented another face to him – a face of kindness to little children.

Presently he became aware that the other inhabitants of the foul-smelling chamber had congregated to watch their sister pay her debt and become a solemn mystery. Their faces were dull and incurious, they might have been watching a cat or a horse; only their blistered and dirty hands, twisting and clenching and wiping away at their skirts betrayed any deeper concern.

Suddenly there was a stirring of interest. Chops's ma had opened her eyes, which did not at all resemble pots of jam, but rather the empty vessels from which all the jam had been spooned away.

'*O Almighty God, with whom do live the spirits,*' Martin began to read quickly, when the word 'spirits' elevated Chops's ma to brighter heights of comprehension. She struggled to raise herself as, dimly through the poisonous fog of gin that Briskitt's homage had enabled her to buy, she perceived a figure at her side.

'Oozee?'

'It's the chapling, you silly cow,' her friend enlightened her, with a warning shake of the head, as if enjoining on her a standard of behaviour beyond the ordinary.

'*... of just men made perfect, after they are delivered from their earthly prisons,*' continued Martin softly, as the woman nodded to him, confirming that Chops's ma was as ready for her voyage as ever she was likely to be.

'Prizzins? Men . . . men?' inquired Chops's ma, dazed and alarmed. 'Wassee on abaht?'

'It's a prair, you drunken 'eethen.'

'Prair? That's all ri' then! Don't want no men . . . 'ad me bellyful . . . he-he! But 'ee said spirits. Can't pay for 'em . . . not till 'ee comes agin . . . Ah! Luvverly li'l bleeder 'ee was! Gimme jools an' flahrs . . . and all them pahnds! Must 'ave bin rich as ol' Nick! I'll pay yer when 'ee comes agin! Briskitt – Briskitt!' she howled suddenly, like a lost soul.

'Shut yer noise an' let the chapling 'ave 'is say!'

But it was too late. Somebody had let the snakes in again; they were crawling up the walls and dropping down on the bed. Dirty little wriggling black things that froze the arse off you when they tried to sting you in the eyes. She kicked and screamed and shrieked as the indelicate reptiles persisted in making inroads into the deepest recesses of her person. Then somebody said somewhere: *'Precious in thy sight'*, in a voice of astonishing gentleness, and she paused to wonder what it could mean? What was precious, and in whose sight? Could it have been that silver locket and chain that she'd sold? But before she could apply herself to this problem, the voice said something about a Lamb. Instantly she thought of a lamb chop, and then, with a great rush of maternal feeling, of Chops.

'My baby!' she howled. 'I want me baby! I want 'im – I want 'im!'

Following this great effusion of tenderness, she was a little sick and then closed her eyes and indicated that she was asleep by snoring with the grim, raucous sound of a saw grating against an iron nail.

'You can nod off, if you like,' said the angel of pity from the opposite bed. 'I'll give yer a nudge if anything 'appens.'

Martin thanked her, but continued with his watching over the dying woman. A wax candle had been provided in honour of the occasion and it shed a sombre radiance over Chops's ma, softening the stains and filth in which she lay, and even restoring to her a sense of mystery.

He found himself staring at her mouth, which hung open making a black moon in her pallid face. Confusedly he recalled the staymaker's maxim, that women's mouths were the windows of their souls . . . which were not souls in the generally accepted sense . . .

Larger and larger grew her mouth, until it engulfed her face and continued to increase until all the room was one huge mouth. Cautiously Martin stepped inside it and began to call, in the dull red cavern, for her soul to come out and be saved. His voice echoed and echoed back again, most curiously in the tones of Orpheus Jones: 'Love on her lips is straying . . .'

But her lips were a long way behind him and he was in the garden which was filled with rapid children. What were they doing? He wandered deeper and deeper, trying to remember all the time that he was not there to enjoy himself but to catch an escaping soul.

To distract him, there were pretty girls dancing in the trees. No! They were dancing *from* the trees! They were hanging by their necks, suspended from nooses of silver chain . . .

'Charity – charity!' cried Dr Dormann, with a tray suspended from his shoulders on which were pewter medallions offered for sale. 'Buy one and save a pretty girl . . . buy one and save poor Fanny Bush! Here, you sir! Wake your ideas up or she'll be gone! Wake up – wake up!'

Martin shut his book and, one by one, the watchers round the bed drifted away; they were wearied of waiting to see Chops's ma gathered to her Father in heaven. No one wanted her . . . not even God. Only her neighbour – the self-appointed angel of pity – remained.

She felt genuinely sorry for the chaplain, sitting there, waiting to get his prayer in before it was too late. She wondered if it would count against him somewhere if he missed his chance? It didn't seem right that the poor holy sod should cop it on account of Chops's ma.

'She brung it on 'erself,' she murmured, in an effort of consolation. 'Silly cow!'

Then, seating herself on the end of her own bed, she confided Chops's ma's base ingratitude towards Briskitt, that generous provider. With misty reverence she told of the gold and jewels and red roses that the ardent swain had brought . . . and the cruel fate he had met with. And Briskitt, his satin waistcoat notwithstanding, was no more than a poor little bleeder like the others, working his fingers to the bone in the Mulberry Garden. It was a downright wicked thing that Chops's ma had done to take his treasures and throw his love back in his face; and she was being punished for it, so that if she did slip her hook before the chaplain could finish his prayer, it was nobody's fault but her own.

At about half past eleven – it was long after dark – the prison governor paid a visit. He stared down at the snoring woman, copiously washed his hands of all responsibility, declared it was a damned conspiracy to discredit him but that he would get to the bottom of it . . . and asked if Martin would honour him with his presence over a bite of supper. Martin shook his head and the governor went away, feeling obscurely that even the man of God was against him.

'Wake up! Wake up!' urged the angel of pity, shaking Martin till his book fell from his lap onto the floor with a rush and a thud.

For a moment Martin fancied he was still caught in his garden dream – a faint but unmistakable smell of earth and trees was in the room – then the fantasy dissolved and he was confronted by a scene that was, in its way, no less fantastic.

The woman's child had returned from his labours in the Mulberry Garden and was crouching on the end of her bed. He was amazingly scratched and filthy and looked, in the candlelight, like some small wild animal that had darted out of the undergrowth. His mother, under the pressure of some frightful dream, had kicked off every scrap of covering, and the child was staring with profound curiosity at the darkness from which he had issued. In addition to this curiosity, there was a touch of melancholy anger and bitterness; Chops, in his youthful simplicity, was blaming the stony-hearted Briskitt for his impending loss.

'I told 'im,' whispered the friend opposite, 'I told 'im that she were kickin' the bucket.'

Chops, overhearing the solemn whisper, turned to stare at Martin. At once, the face leaped out of Martin's memory. Distorted by malevolence though it had been at the time, he recognized in Chops the child who had spied on him through the railings of Fanny Bush's basement! Involuntarily he shrank from the child from the Mulberry Garden, the tiny watcher . . .

'They'll look arter 'im,' pursued the friend gently. 'The garden. Lots of 'em like 'im there.'

Martin's heart leaped with understanding as a host of disconnected recollections crept, like mice, out of the dark corners of his mind! The child sleeping in the church;

children appearing and vanishing as if in and out of holes in the air; children with bright, sharp eyes, children in the garden . . .

'Briskitt told her to go to hell,' muttered Chops miserably, 'and now she's going.'

'She'll go straight to 'eaven, dearie,' comforted the angel of pity. 'She'll go right up like a bleedin' puff o' smoke. You tell 'im, chapling.'

Martin hesitated. The realization that had just come to him had disturbed and excited him considerably, but there was no time at the present moment to dwell upon it. He pushed it from his mind and did what he could to assure the child that, henceforth, his mother would be watching over him all the time.

But, to Chops, watching meant spying, even as he spied himself, so the concept, far from comforting him, alarmed him still further. Like all children, Chops, though he delighted in peeping into the worlds of others, was himself a secretive little soul . . . He began to cry; his tiny body heaved and shook, and mournful howls of astonishing volume filled the gloomy room; dim faces arose out of the shadows of sleep and glimmered half resentfully at the wailing object that had disturbed them . . .

Martin leaned forward to lay a hand on Chops's shoulder, but the child moved away and attempted to enfold himself in his mother's unresponding arms. Martin, watching this, found himself remembering the scroundrelly old man who had paid for the privilege of stealing pity because it gave him warmth. Again he felt that that was what it all came down to: the need for warmth. First and last – warmth. Nothing else really mattered . . .

As he sat helplessly by the bed, he tried to strike a bargain with God or the devil (whichever one would listen) that he would surrender his priceless gift – supposing he still possessed it – to be of some service to Chops and his ma. It seemed to him at that time that the loss of this stinking wreckage of a woman was more grievous and more important than the fall of an empire . . .

'She's woke up!' exclaimed the angel of pity. 'Look! 'e's woke 'er up!'

Chops's ma had opened her eyes. From that remote region to which she had retired, borne on a river of burning gin, she had heard the voice of her offspring and drifted back to gaze upon him.

'Didjer bring 'im? Luvverly li'l Briskitt?'

Chops shook his head.

'Didjer tell 'im I was porly? Didjer tell 'im abaht the 'ug'na kiss?'

Chops nodded and his ma, incredulous and horribly dismayed that her charms had been rejected, dragged up the strength to declare that Briskitt was the nastiest little bleeder she had ever come across and that she hoped that all his important parts would drop off and be eaten by the rats.

Martin shuddered as he heard the dying woman heap her frightful primitive curses on a child; he tried to calm her down by continuing with the prayer he had begun, but she only wanted Briskitt, Briskitt and what his riches might bring . . .

Then Chops, his rage and hatred against his iron-hearted patron mounting, took vengeance into his own hands. Impatient for his mother's curses to take effect, he set about betraying Briskitt and all the nefarious concerns he knew or guessed about to the gentleman who represented a higher power even than Dr Dormann – a gentleman who was well in with the hereafter.

He told of Briskitt's pride and Briskitt's cunning, of

Briskitt's vanity and meanness, of Briskitt's wealth and the mysterious meetings on Fridays from whence that wealth came. Weeping with bitterness he told of his own fears that Briskitt might have been knifed – like that other one – and that now he prayed with all his heart and soul that, on this coming Friday, Briskitt would meet with the fate he so richly deserved. For there was no one who would miss Briskitt, not even Mrs Bray, who could easily find a better child to take Briskitt's place on the twelfth arbour and look down . . .

All this Martin heard with a dazed comprehension. He longed to question the child further, but the time, the distressful room and his own feelings of pity forbade him, and he was forced to let the opportunity escape him.

Shortly before dawn, Chops slipped from his mother's arms and fell to the floor. He picked himself up and peered inquisitively into the quiet face; then, turning to Martin with an expression of deep triumph, he said: 'She's dozed off proper, now.'

Martin trembled; he supposed that the woman had died. But it was not so; the dreadful, metallic snoring had given way to a soft and regular breathing. Although it was impossible for her to survive for very long, the immediate danger was past. Chops beamed at him.

'Thank you, mister.'

'But I –' began Martin, anxious to disclaim any gratitude for a change he had done nothing to bring about.

'– If you should come across Briskitt,' said Chops, interrupting him, 'you can tell him from me that it's all right now.'

Chops's resentment had evaporated and he was concerned to restore himself into the good graces of his admired friend.

'How will I know him? Where will I find him?'

Chops grinned. 'Easy, mister. He's been following you for days!'

Chapter Eighteen

So at last Martin became aware of the children, of the little children. As he left the gaol, a tremendous excitement took hold of him; the revelations that had been made and Chops's betrayal of Briskitt filled him with a totally unexpected hope. He must find Briskitt. Briskitt had the knowledge that could save him and save Fanny Bush from the peril in which she stood. He groaned aloud in misery at the thought of it. That he, of all people, should have delivered her, innocent and helpless, into the hand of the Mulberry Garden and the devil!

But that was all behind him now; he had only to find Briskitt ...

'Briskitt – Briskitt!' he called out as he heard footsteps following him. But the grey street was empty and they had been footsteps in his tired mind.

He returned to his house and slept until past noon; then he resumed his search. At first his hopes remained high, but, little by little, as the hours passed and night came on, he began to feel that he was opposing forces that must inevitably defeat him. The very knowledge that he had gained seemed to have turned against him and become a weapon in another's hands. It was a curious but undoubted fact that, since he had uncovered the garden's ramifications and the strange activities of its children, children themselves seemed to have vanished from his sight.

Whereas before the streets had been alive with them, now they were nowhere to be seen; he walked, he felt, in a world without children. Yet he felt that every shadow concealed them, every corner and doorway stirred with them and their rapid footfalls were always in his ears; but when he turned, however quickly, there was – nothing!

Once or twice he did actually succeed in catching a child full in his sight.

'Briskitt?' he asked pleadingly. 'Are you Briskitt?' But the child only shook its head blankly and scuttled away.

He began to feel that he was searching for a puff of smoke and that, even if he did find it, it would disperse into the air like a stain with an acrid smell. Several times he contemplated returning to the garden which was, after all, the lair of Briskitt; but the place had become terrifying and hateful to him now that he knew that every private act within it was watched by countless gleeful eyes. Besides, what chance would he have of finding one tiny Satan among a whole hellful?

Yet again and again he told himself he *must* find Briskitt – the child who almost certainly *knew*.

What manner of child was this Briskitt who carried around in his head the knowledge of the worst sin in the world? Briskitt was proud, Chops had said, and Briskitt was cunning; Briskitt was rich and Briskitt had a heart of stone. An image, not unlike the abominable Sir David Brown, only smaller, came into Martin's mind. Briskitt was the distillation of evil in the shape of a child, such as any self-respecting Scottish saint would have booted into the widest firth or the deepest loch without more ado. Briskitt had horns and a tail and was smoked in sulphur like a kipper ...

'Briskitt? Are you Briskitt?' demanded Martin hopelessly of a melancholy child in Peartree Court on the Wednesday morning.

Instantly the child turned to marble; became, as it were, a stony replica of a child, flawed with scratches and dirt.

'Oo?'

'Briskitt – Briskitt?'

156

'Nar,' said Briskitt. 'Never!'

'Briskitt!' cried Martin, guessing, by the child's abject terror, that his quest was ended. 'There's no need to be frightened of me,' he said, his voice trembling with excitement. 'I know everything about you . . .'

The stone that was Briskitt began to melt and tremble; he uttered a low moan. To be told, in one and the same breath, that everything was known about him and not to be frightened, seemed to him an unholy contradiction. 'You got the wrong boy, mister. On me bible oaf!'

'I have a message for you, Briskitt; from a friend.'

'I told yer,' groaned Briskitt. 'I give yer me solumm oaf, as Gawd's me witness an' may 'e strike me dahn wiv a fevver, it's not me name!'

Martin gazed on the distillation of evil in the shape of a child and saw that he was plainly searching for some hole in the ground into which he might conveniently make a retreat. Briskitt's horns were a threadbare cap of dirty hair, pulled out in tufts by thorns so that his scalp showed up in islands; Briskitt's tail was a bedraggled garment that hung in a long tatter behind him; and Briskitt's smell was not of sulphur but of loneliness, bewilderment and fear.

'The message, Briskitt. Will you hear it?'

Briskitt, finding no hole in the ground nor other exit from the empty court, hesitated. After all, he had nothing to lose by listening, and it was just possible that the message might be important and concern his source of income. He brooded on what course it behove him to take, on how he might obtain the message without yielding anything of the position he had taken up. At length, with much wrinkling of the brow and scratching of the head, he suggested, circuitously, that if the message was given to *him*, who was not, under any circumstances, Briskitt, he would do his very best to pass it on. He couldn't say fairer than that.

'That's very kind of you,' said Martin, who couldn't find it in his heart to strip Briskitt naked, there and then.

'The message is from a boy whose mother is very ill in Bridewell Gaol. The message to Briskitt is, that everything is all right now.'

'Ah!' thought Briskitt reproachfully, 'Chops has betrayed me yet again!' His indignation knew no bounds, for Chops had already informed on him to Dr Dormann and he had only been able to extricate himself from the doctor's fierce questioning by a mixture of stark obstinacy and brilliant lying. And now the rotten little bleeder had done it again! 'I'll pull his poxy little arms and legs off,' vowed Briskitt. 'One by bleeding one I'll have 'em off. So help me God.'

'I'll pass the noos on,' said Briskitt, and prepared to depart.

'But that's not all.'

'Oh?'

'Can I talk to you . . . about Briskitt?'

Briskitt considered. Escape was still denied him; and, after all, what had he got to lose?

'I fink I ken spare yer a minnit or two,' he said. Martin thanked him.

'Shall we sit on that step?' he suggested, pointing to the projecting entrance of a cellar. Briskitt shrugged his shoulders and the man and boy seated themselves side by side under the noonday sun. The court was silent, and the bricked-up windows seemed only just to have closed their eyes on the scene as watcher and watched contemplated their feet.

'Do you remember the murder in the Mulberry Garden?'

Briskitt rose to go.

'You said it was abaht Briskitt, mister.'

'Yes, it is about Briskitt,' said Martin quietly. 'It's about Briskitt who works and watches in the garden and about what Briskitt saw on a certain Friday.'

Then the proximity of the child, whom he could feel trembling beside him, gave him a sense of warmth and power so that words came almost unbidden to his lips.

'It's about Briskitt and the money and gifts he used to bring to the lady in Bridewell Gaol. It's about Briskitt who must have loved with all his heart, and then come to hate with all his strength. It's really all about Briskitt. Everything is about Briskitt . . .'

Briskitt seemed to shrink as he crouched deeper and deeper into his own shadow. He peered up at Martin as if from an immense distance.

'Owjer know that? Was it 'er what let on?'

'No . . . no. It wasn't her. I heard things, of course . . . but it really wasn't her.'

'Owjer know then? Oo let on?'

'It – it was me, myself. It was pity, and – and fear . . . and shame and love . . . and – and –'

'You got one too, mister, ain't yer? You got a woman.'

'Yes. I suppose so . . .'

'They're wicked. Tear yer guts aht. I'm done wiv 'em.'

Even as Chops had said, Briskitt's heart had turned to stone. With tight-lipped dignity he had remained unmoved by every blandishment; and even the mysterious delights the damsel had intimated might be his if he relented had failed to move him from his solemn course of never no more.

'Never no more,' said Briskitt. 'Never no more.'

'Then what will you do?'

Briskitt shook his head and his eyes began to swim with dreams. He began to confide in Martin that henceforth his wealth (and he wasn't saying where it came from) was to be devoted to his own advancement. He was going to make something of himself. He was going to set himself up and become independent.

'And yer know wot I mean by that,' said the small misogynist, with a twisted smile.

'How will you do it?'

Briskitt looked wise. He had seen a pair of globes in a shop window in Compton Street. On one had been depicted the world, and on the other, the heavens. There had been ships and beasts and angels all over them and, in addition, empty scrolls on which the purchaser's name and crest were to be recorded with dignity and elegance. They came to twenty-five pounds the pair and Briskitt considered them a sensible purchase for one in his situation. They were, as was said, a work of art and an heirloom such as would grace any home. They were an *investment*.

Martin listened and marvelled at the innocence of Briskitt who had looked down on darkness and secrets and the worst of crimes. Far from the innocence being corrupted by the sight of guilt, the guilt itself seemed to have been transfigured by innocence. So it must be with the angels, looking down . . . What *was* the garden?

'An' I'll tell yer anuvver fing, mister,' continued Briskitt, pleased with Martin and finding him an infinitely worthier repository for confidences than Chops. 'This Fridy's me last. I'll get me twenty-five pahnds an' call it a night. Old Dormann'll be onto it an' then Mrs Bray an' I'll be aht on me arse.'

'I'll give you the twenty-five pounds now,' said Martin eagerly. 'Tell me who it is!'

Briskitt shook his head. 'I'd like to, mister. I'd sooner you than Dr Dormann. But I give me solumm oaf. Arter all, 'e's paid me up till now.'

'So it is a man! You must tell me! I *must* know. Listen – I know already about the dress and that there was no coat! I know the one who was killed was wearing the dress. Please tell me everything!'

Briskitt was visibly amazed by the extent of Martin's knowledge; but still he shook his head, and clung obstinately to the importance of his solemn oath.

'Then will you tell me why? Do you know why it was done?'

Briskitt shrugged his shoulders. 'It were just a lark, if you arsk me. Could 'ave knocked me dahn wiv a fevver when the knife went in. You 'ad to larf, though.'

'Yes . . . yes, you really are innocent,' said Martin, with a mixture of gratitude and hopelessness in his voice.

Briskitt looked puzzled. The word 'innocent' was not a part of his vocabulary. Either you were 'fahnd aht', or 'not fahnd aht'; the rest was mere philosophy.

'Garn!' he said. 'Get on wiv yer!'

'Then you'll tell me no more?'

Briskitt thought deeply. Many considerations needed to be taken into account. He liked Martin; there was no doubt that the gent had a gift for getting on with you. He sort of *eased* things out of you and made you feel better for it, whereas Dr Dormann went at it with a carving knife and left you feeling like it. But, on the other hand, he had given his solemn oath. Then again, on the *other* hand (Briskitt was a spider when it came to hands), there was the twenty-five pounds and heaven and earth waiting in Compton Street. You really had to think of everything.

'Tell you what, mister. If I don't get me twenty-five

pahnd on Fridy, then I'll come to you. 'E knows that if 'e don't pay up, 'e's got to take 'is chances. Is it a bargin, mister? Twenty-five pahnd?'

'It's a bargain, Briskitt!'

'You'll be there on Fridy?'

'Yes – yes!'

''Ow will I know yer?'

'What do you mean?'

'Masks, mister. Last Fridy in the month. Masks.'

'I'll – I'll be wearing these clothes.'

'Then it's till Fridy, mister. That is, maybe.'

Chapter Nineteen

MASKS, masks – a garden full of masks! Masks of black
silk fringed with lace, masks of midnight blue ... Masks
with green sequins and masks encrusted with brilliants so
that the turning countenances, catching in the lantern-
light, blazed up like heads of stars!

Silvery masks and golden masks, and masks with great
white lashes stitched round the eye-slits, like exploded
chrysanthemums with hearts as black as the Friday night.

'*Love in her eyes sits playing,*' warbled the masked tenor
from the rotunda; and all the ladies' eyes rolled and
turned, leaving only the red, red mouths to part and smile
and pout for kisses, necessary as air.

'Who's that? Who *are* you? Let me see you!'

'I'd know you anywhere!' breathed a mask of the very best black worsted at nineteen shillings the yard.

'Would you? *Would* you?' returned a mouth he thought he knew, but suddenly, with a thrill, wondered if he really did?

Carnival masks – large painted faces of cats and lions and grinning demons – came winding in, with nods and hops and strange gyrations of stalking legs and waving arms to frighten the ladies into shrieks and screams and spillings of the garden's wine. Masked waiters hastened to and fro, to mop them up and fill the glasses again.

And up in the trees, and nesting in the arbours, little masked children peered down; for Mrs Bray who was, in all but size, a child herself, had made them all little green masks, like leaves.

'Mouths are the windows of their souls!' thought Martin, seeing Fanny Bush in her garden gown, and wearing a mask of the same material.

She was all flowers, and her mouth made a smile of pleasure as Martin, deeply masked in black, came towards her.

'I'd know you anywhere,' she murmured. 'You've got such a kind mouth!'

'All the better to eat you with!' grinned a carnival mask, interposing between them, and glaring from one to the other.

Martin stared into the monster's rolling eyes. Who was it?

'Be off with you!' laughed Fanny. 'Go frighten some children!' and she pushed the intruder away.

Martin watched him stalk and stumble off, and aggravate every table he came to, and at last vanish into the garden's dark. Was it *him*? Was he the one that Briskitt was to meet? He stared up among the lantern-lit branches. Would Briskitt come to him? He had money with him . . . money enough for everything.

'Briskitt . . . Briskitt!' he breathed, as if he was uttering a prayer.

'Oo's there?'

The masked Briskitt, crouching on the edge of the lake-pit, looked up. A figure, blacker than the night, stood above him. He wore a nightmare for a face, with eyes like burning wheels of fire.

'Izzat you?' asked Briskitt, uneasily. The figure remained absolutely motionless and was glaring down at him something terrible. '*Izzit*?'

'Who are you?'

'Me? Oh! I see!'

Briskitt chuckled with relieved understanding. He took off his green mask and presented his small, eager face to the nightmare.

'Well? *Izzit* you?'

'Yes.'

'Gimme quite a turn . . . comin' up soft as a bleedin' ghost.'

'Did I frighten you?'

'Not now you don't.'

'I'm glad of that. I don't want to frighten children . . . as well.'

'Oo else is there, then?'

'Myself.'

'Garn! You're 'avin' me on! Tell yer wot, though! I got good noos.'

'What is it? What good news can *you* have?'

''Old on. No need to get nasty. I got bad noos as well.'

'I don't doubt it.'

'Dontcher want to 'ear?'

'Yes. Tell me your . . . news.'

'Good noos fust, then. Arter this time, I'm goin' to call it a night. Straight up – it'll be the finish. Now that's good noos, ain't it?'

'That's good news. What of the bad news?'

'Baad noos is, I want twenty-five pahnds.'

'But – but I haven't got it!' said the nightmare in a voice that suddenly shook with fear.

'An' I got to 'av it,' said Briskitt regretfully. 'If I don't, you're fer the chop, me lad! I can't 'elp meself. I give me solumm oaf.'

'Then somebody else knows?' The nightmare's face remained unchanged, but its hands had begun to twist and turn.

'Good noos an' bad noos agin,' said Briskitt, watching the hands carefully. 'Good noos is, nobody knows. Bad noos is, that it won't be long afore they do. That's why tonight's me last. Straight up! Cross me 'eart an' 'ope to be struck dahn wiv a fevver.'

'You must give me time – time!' pleaded the nightmare. 'I'll bring you the money! I swear it!'

'I told yer,' said Briskitt firmly, 'it's got to be nar or you're fer the chop. I give me solumm oaf, yer know.'

'Please – please give me more time!' The nightmare's hands had come together in anguished supplication.

But the heartless little demon in the pit was adamant; Briskitt's soul was fixed upon the globes in Compton Street.

'Look – look! Here's a watch! It's gold – I swear it! It must be worth – worth twice what you want! Take it – take it!'

Briskitt peered with interest at the watch that swung on a fine chain before his eyes. It was gold all right. He looked up at the nightmare, and suddenly began to grin.

'What is it?'

'I was jus' finkin'. You when you stuck your knife in. Your fice. Larf? I nearly died!'

'Not nearly enough!' whispered the nightmare, and dropped the watch.

''Ere! You'll spoil it! Gimme ... 'ere! 'ere! Wot yer up to? Piss off, will yer?'

But Briskitt had been taken unawares. Quick as a stinking, bloody viper, a pair of hands had come out and got him by the neck. He tried to kick, to claw at the suffocating fingers; but they were like iron. 'Chops was right', thought Briskitt, as the nightmare's face bent close over him and the eyes began to turn like cartwheels going down a hill, ''e's goin' to do me in!'

'You're 'urtin' – you're 'urtin' me! I can't breeve!' he tried to scream; but nothing came except a small grunting noise that Briskitt could hardly believe was all there was left.

He could feel his tongue coming out by the roots and all the world went round and round with a whistle and a shriek. Then he saw the face of death. Or worse than that: the ghost of Mr Bray. There was no doubt about it; it was bony all over with black holes for eyes and teeth like area railings painted white.

'Leave him!' he heard death say. 'Leave him and come with me.'

The nightmare jerked back, and Briskitt began to fall. Down, down he rushed, clawed at by bushes and roots till he struck earth in the black depths of the pit.

'You – you 'urt me!' he panted, as he rolled over. 'You 'urt me!' he sobbed as he stared up, through mists of shock and pain, to where the death's head and the nightmare stood, grinning down.

'Come with me,' murmured the death's head.

'Where? Where?' asked the nightmare.

'Out of the garden . . .'

Briskitt lay very still; his eyes were shut and he might have been dead and in his grave. Insects crawled over him and made meals in his hair; everything was against him – the small no less than the great. He opened his eyes and saw the edge of the pit and the grim black sky beyond, where the stars pointed down like arrows.

They had gone; the nightmare and the death's head had departed. Briskitt began to crawl up. His throat was grievously sore and he found it painful even to draw breath. Presently he reached the place from which he'd been thrown down; he began to search and scrabble in the earth and among the sharp roots of bushes that clawed at him like children's hands. Suddenly he grunted. He had found the watch.

'Briskitt!'

'Gerroff!' croaked Briskitt, in a paroxysm of rage and dread.

'I guessed it . . . it would be here,' said Martin, coming to kneel down beside the boy. 'Did he come?'

'Get away! Get away!' snarled Briskitt, uttering the words with immense difficulty. His late experience had left him with a terror and hatred of everything. All that mattered, in heaven and earth, was the gold watch.

'What happened?'

Briskitt didn't answer; all he wanted was to escape and crawl into some dark and private place and plan hideous revenges on the world that had so maltreated him.

'Did he give you what you wanted?'

Briskitt held up the watch.

'He gave it to you? Let me see it!'

'No yer bleedin' don't! Said it were werf . . . lots . . .'

'Give it to me! I'll give you money –'

'Said . . . it were – were werf . . . more'n twent-five . . . much more . . . double, 'e said. . . .'

'Here! Take this purse! Look! There's plenty here! More than enough to buy those globes you want! Take it, Briskitt, and go and buy your – your world and heavens in Compton Street! See – see how much there is!'

'Gimme –' snarled Briskitt, baring his sharp teeth like a wild dog. He snatched the purse and threw down the watch.

'Briskitt! Briskitt, child!' cried out Martin; but Briskitt had gone.

He went like a sudden, rushing wind. Bruised in every limb, with aching neck and rasping breath, he ran down the long, tunnelled paths, cursing the masked faces that turned to make startled mouths at him. Not knowing altogether from what, he ran for dear life . . . although to call it dear was not, in Briskitt's case, entirely truthful. At last he reached the gate and, with a final raucous grunt, he fled out of the garden for ever.

All was lost to him; he knew it with certainty. He had no choice but to go like this, or to suffer the last indignity of being violently cast out.

Ferociously he clutched the full purse; but his heart was empty. Not even the glorious globes of heaven and earth – the heirloom that would grace any home – lightened his darkness. He didn't want them any more. Where could he have kept them – what could he have done with them? They were toys for children, and all that was behind him.

He paused in his flight and stared back towards the garden and saw, as in a receding dream, the cobwebby world of moths and beetles and birds and the glimmering paradise on which he'd looked down; he remembered the strange nursery of Mrs Bray. . .

'Never no more!' wept Briskitt, and ran on and on into the night. 'Never no more!'

In the Mulberry Garden Martin hastened back to the rotunda. Eagerly he examined the watch under the lantern light, turning it this way and that with mounting excitement. The back was engraved. He had seen it dimly when Briskitt had held it up. He could make out a name; but it meant nothing to him. Below this was an address: Salisbury Court . . .

'Where are you going?' asked Fanny, obscurely frightened by Martin's look.

He stared at her, wildly and imploringly.

'Wait! Wait for me!' he pleaded.

'How long must I wait?'

But Martin had gone; he had rushed from the garden like a madman.

Chapter Twenty

SALISBURY COURT was a deep, quiet socket of a place, approached from Dorset Street by a narrow passage called The Wilderness. The houses were tall and cheek by jowl, forming an exclusive community of shadows into which a dim intrusion was achieved by a single lamp placed on the corner of The Wilderness. At low tide – for the river was near – the air was motionless and distinctly dank; at high tide, owing to various odd configurations of stone and brick, a wind seemed to breathe through, smelling and sounding of the sea. At times, it seemed as if the whole court was a convoluted shell, pressed to an invisible ear.

'Charming . . . charming,' murmured the death's head to the nightmare. 'You are to be envied . . . living here. Do you know, I believe I can smell the sea?'

'It's the river. It's at high tide.'

Forgetful of their masks, they stood under the lamp on the corner of The Wilderness, the death's head tall and lean, and the nightmare broad-shouldered and inclined to be squat.

They had come by cab and occasioned much merriment to the driver who had kept peering back inside his vehicle and then making witty remarks to his horse to the effect that he didn't ought to have taken that last glass of gin as he was seeing things.

Throughout the journey, which had taken some fifteen minutes, his two extraordinary passengers had not exchanged a single word with one another; they had occupied opposite seats and stared away at one another with the fixed expressions of terror and death.

'Ah! The river!' sighed the death's head, turning his

grin this way and that, as he savoured the air. '"*The water of the river shall become blood"*', as it says in the Scriptures. What a wonderful book it is! A thought for every day . . . for every minute, if one thinks about it. You read the Bible, of course? I can see by the sort of clothes you wear that you are a cultured man.'

'What are you going to do? What do you want? For God's sake come out with it! I tell you, I'm at the end of my tether! I've been going through hell!'

The voice, proceeding from behind the nightmare's painted howl, was low and harsh and gave way, under stress, to odd lapses in the pronunciation of certain words.

'I only want to help you,' whispered the death's head, earnestly. 'Please believe me . . .'

'Will you come into my house? It's there . . . opposite.'

'Come into my parlour, eh? No, no! I'm sorry! I didn't really mean that! The words just slipped out. And anyway, I can see that your servants are still up. You would hardly ask me in, meaning to do something terrible, with servants about?'

'Servants? Oh! I see. The light. I don't have any servants. It's just that I don't like coming back to the dark,' said the nightmare.

'I can understand that,' said the death's head eagerly. 'I also have feelings about the dark and I'm delighted to hear you admit to them. That's an honest thing to do and it puts me at my ease at once. Of course we must go inside . . . and thank you very much for inviting me!'

The two strange figures, both dressed neatly in black, which contrasted derisively with their large, mad faces, crossed the court and entered a house with a light shining from an upper window.

They climbed to the first floor and went into a parlour that overlooked the corner of The Wilderness.

'What a charming room and such a delightful view! You must spend many happy hours here. It is quite a retreat from the noisy world. I can imagine it – surrounded by one's books . . . the Bible, of course! One can really be a philosopher in a room like this!'

'For God's sake, tell me what you want!' moaned the nightmare, sinking into a chair and clutching his mask with his hands, but making no effort to remove it. 'I can't stand any more of this bloody chatter! You said you could 'elp . . . er help me? Then do it before I go mad!'

The death's head raised up his large white hands in an almost comical gesture of apology and dismay. Then he turned his great grin on the oil lamp that stood upon the table.

'Look! A moth! Just let me save it if I can. Moths are souls, you know. I used to be told that when I was a child; and I still partly believe it! There, now! It's still alive! Isn't it fortunate that we came in when we did? We've saved a soul from burning! Now shall we see if we can save another? What do you say to this? Sit down – sit down!' This as the nightmare half rose, in a fit of trembling.

'I have a friend, sir . . . a cultured gentleman –'

'Don't talk about your damned friends! I've asked you – for God's sake, to come out with it! What are you? *Who* are you?'

'Oh yes, of course! We're still wearing masks,' said Dr Dormann, lifting up his death's head with a pale and somewhat fearful smile.

'So . . . so, it's you,' he said, as his companion took off one nightmare to reveal another.

The face was that of the ugly man who always sat alone. It was a face that looked to have been wrenched out of shape; it was unequal in everything and created a sense of sickness and revulsion in the beholder. It was, most likely, an injury sustained at birth . . . perhaps a careless midwife's fingers had fumbled and distorted the soft tissue . . . ?

'You're a priest!' said the ugly one, his eyes fixed on Dr Dormann's Geneva bands, which had been concealed by his mask.

'Certainly I am a student of divinity . . . in the widest sense, that is. I read a great deal in my youth, you understand. Learned commentaries and all that sort of thing. Oh, I assure you, churches, chapels and synagogues are no strangers to me! Disputing with the doctors and all that! Will you confess to me?'

'Confess? Confess? I can't confess! Oh for God's sake, help me!'

'I will – I will! That's why you must confess to me! Don't you see how much better it will be? There'll be no secret any more! It will be mine, not yours; and I'll guard it with my life! I give you my word of honour. You must look at it this way . . . what you did was done in the garden. It belongs to the garden. Nobody else will know. You must trust the garden. Many, many do. Confess to me now and – pay me fifty pounds. (You *have* fifty pounds? But of course! You're a man of means . . . I can see that! The furnishings and your clothes!) Pay me fifty pounds and that will be an end of it. The payment is quite necessary . . . as much for you as for the garden. You will know, you see . . . How shall I explain it? It will be a transaction. You will have paid for peace of mind . . . But it's the confession that really matters! My dear sir, I implore you – confess, and then see how much better it is!'

The ugly man sat staring at Dr Dormann in horrible incredulity. His hands kept clenching and unclenching in a way that made Dr Dormann fear an outburst of violence. He *was* a violent fellow, there was no doubt of it. He had almost killed that child . . .

Suddenly the ugly man reared up and Dr Dormann involuntarily shrank away. But the man was not going to attack him. He gave a deep cry and stumbled out of the room. He was gone only for seconds. He rushed back in again.

'Look! Look at this!' he sobbed, and held out the grey and yellow muslin gown that clung against him as if he was wearing it.

'All right – all right! I did it! I stabbed him! I pushed that knife in 'im ... in *him*, I mean, as hard as I could! I had it in my hand! I'd been peeling an orange with it. It was still wet from the juice! It went in him up to the handle. I couldn't get it any further. He couldn't believe it! He looked ... *surprised* ...'

'Was it – was it because of *the crime against nature*?' whispered Dr Dormann, as the floodgates of confession suddenly opened up.

'Crime against nature? You're mad! It was nature's crime ... against me ... against *me*! He was wearing it – this dress! I didn't know ... he was padded out or something! He came up to me, smiling. He was beautiful, I tell you! I'd never seen anything like it! I didn't know what to make of him! I'd no idea, I'd no *idea* that it was ... him! As God's my witness –'

'And He always is,' put in Dr Dormann softly. 'It's best to think so.'

'I never knew – I never guessed!'

'So that's why you ... did it?'

'I must tell you – I must tell you the worst of it! Can I put back my mask? Please, let me wear it? Thank you – thank you! He came right up to me ... smiling and making mouths. Then he said – for pity's sake don't laugh – he said I was what she – he had been searching for all her life! I swear it was said! The words have been in my ears ever since! So ... so I knelt ... yes, I *knelt down*, in front of him. I must have seen a painting once, of a knight kneeling to his lady! Don't smile at me! Please look away! And then – and then when she'd got me to kneel down, she . . . *he* lifted up his dress and showed me how I'd been deceived! That's why I did it, you know! The *pretence*!'

The nightmare collapsed back in his chair, quite exhausted. Dr Dormann rose and fumbled in his pocket. He produced a pewter medallion. 'Go fetch the fifty pounds – and take this, my friend. It will give you peace . . . in the garden.'

But the man had not yet finished. There was still more he wanted to unburden himself of; the floodgates, once opened, were not so easily shut.

He ran to a sideboard and, dragging open the cupboard, pulled out a length of rope.

'Look! Look at this! I was going to hang myself with it! I even tried to put a hook in the ceiling! And then I thought, why not go to the magistrate and confess? They'd hang me just the same. But I couldn't. I bought a pistol . . . but the hammer broke! For God's sake don't laugh at me! I really did these things. Then the river. I watched it and was going to jump in. And do you know why I didn't? I thought, as I was standing on that wall next to Whitefriars Stairs – I thought – *I can't swim!* That was yesterday.'

'But now,' said Dr Dormann gently, 'that's all behind you. There's no need now. You've paid your debt. You're quite free.'

'The fifty pounds! Here's the fifty pounds!' panted the nightmare, ransacking a drawer in a desk. 'Take it . . . and God bless you! You were quite right . . . about confessing! It's wonderful! To feel free again! You see – you see . . . I'm really very ordinary in my heart. Perhaps if I wasn't – if I was . . . was as I look, then it would be different. But I'm not, you know! I felt guilt and terror and sickness . . .

and all the time I kept seeing him – her everywhere! I can't believe it's all over! Will I see you again? I want to see you again! Please don't go now . . . stay a little longer. Have some supper with me! Don't hurry away! There's more I want to tell you!'

'I must go now!'

'Why – why – why?'

'Look out of the window. There's someone in the street. He's waiting . . . for me.'

Dr Dormann's voice shook with alarm. Standing under the lamp on the corner of The Wilderness, and staring up at the houses, was Martin Young!

How had he come there? What damnable congregation of chances had led him there? But there was still time . . .

'The dress!' he exclaimed suddenly. 'You must burn it – now! At once! Set fire to it in the grate. Oil . . . pour on some oil. You have oil? Good – good! The dress must be ashes. Nothing left. This is important!'

'Oh I understand that! Look, I'll do it now. If only you'll wait a little while, you can watch it for yourself.'

'No. That's impossible. I have to meet . . . this friend. And we don't want him coming up here, do we? Not *now*. He must never come!'

'Oh God forbid! But will you come back?'

'Perhaps . . . perhaps.'

'Please! I've so much more to tell you. You've no idea of the joy you've given me. You are a wonderful man, sir. I want to talk and talk to you. I'll buy more books . . . you're fond of books, you said. Tell me which ones and we'll read them together, and – and we'll dispute as you did with the doctors! You said you liked this room? Then think of it as another home . . .'

'The oil! Pour on the oil! Anoint it!'

'But you'll come back?'

'Yes – yes! Where is my mask? Ah! Here it is! It's valuable, you see. Pour on more oil! A burning fiery furnace!'

'Ah! That's in the Bible, ain't it?'

'Yes – yes! *"And their garments were cast into the midst of the burning fiery furnace."*'

'As you said, sir, a thought for every day. Perhaps we can read it together?'

'Tomorrow,' said Dr Dormann, and left the room.

While the other had been babbling on, Dr Dormann had been thinking furiously. He must prevent Martin from entering the house before the dress was destroyed and the wretched man had calmed himself and got over his mania for confessing.

He began to descend the dark stairs. He paused, trembling with agitation. Martin was a younger and stronger man. As soon as he saw Dr Dormann leaving the house, he would guess, he would *know*! He would brush him aside like a dead leaf!

Then, suddenly, Dr Dormann smiled and, with the utmost difficulty, prevented himself laughing aloud. Of course – of course!

Chapter Twenty-one

MARTIN rushing out of the Mulberry Garden, clattering down Rag Street, shouting his head off for a cab! Two, three passed him by, with bored, idle, hateful passengers sitting inside, as if their useless journeys could have a fraction of the urgency of *his*! He longed to seize them, to shake them, to pull them out and tell them that he was on a matter of life and death!

A cab stopped for him!

'Salisbury Court! Quickly!'

The horse gazed at him more intelligently than its driver.

'Be that near Salisbury Square, sir?'

'I don't know – I don't know!'

'Or there's a Salisbury Passage, I fancy, off Soho Square? Could Salisbury Court be near there?'

'For God's sake ask someone! Only take me there!'

'Ah! Now I come to recollect, the Soho one ain't Salisbury at all. Somethin' like it, though. I'll take you to Salisbury Square and maybe we can ask.'

Martin in the cab, biting his nails, glaring like a madman at the slowly passing streets and cursing every obstruction.

'Hurry – hurry!'

He couldn't explain to himself this fierce feeling of haste; all he knew was that, somehow, every minute was of the utmost importance. In vain, he tried to calm himself, but the feeling was so strong that it fed upon itself, increasing so that, whenever the cab's pace seemed to diminish, he thrust his head out of the window ready to curse anything that had got in the way.

They reached Salisbury Square. It was empty. There was not a soul to ask.

'I know where it is!' said the driver suddenly. 'It's off Dorset Street!'

Martin blessed him for a geographer of genius, and the cab toppled and ground its way to Dorset Street.

'Through that slit of a way yonder, sir. Too narrow for us, but it ain't far to walk . . .'

Walk? Walk? Martin – running through The Wilderness, and then, halting under the lamp. Salisbury Court stretched before him, quiet as the grave. Blandly the houses ignored him.

He stared from window to window; saw a light here, a light there. Which house? He could see no name plates on the doors. How could he know? How could he know even if he found the right one?

One house in particular kept drawing his attention. It

stood almost directly opposite the lamp and a light was shining from its first-floor front. He watched it closely for several minutes, trying to make up his mind. Suddenly, the light grew brighter, as if a fire had been lit in the room. Yet . . . yet it was a warm night. The fire increased until it was blazing up like a furnace. This was the house!

Shaking with excitement he began to walk towards it, when the door opened and someone came out.

Martin cried out. The figure that had emerged was wearing a huge carnival mask of a death's head; as soon as it saw Martin, it threw up its hands in dismay and fled! It was the man!

With a cry of triumph, Martin pursued . . . while behind him the window of the first floor front danced and blazed away as the fire within steadily reduced something to incomprehensible ash.

The masked figure fled with amazing rapidity. It scampered along the court and vanished into a nest of lanes so that only its scuttling footsteps could be heard. But the interruption was brief and the lanes gave out into a broader thoroughfare.

'Stop him! Stop him!' shouted Martin, as he saw the death's head, with black coat flying like Satan's wings, rushing on ahead.

Two lawyers, returning sedately to the Temple after a late supper, paused at the cry and stared at the extra-ordinary scene.

'Stop him! Stop him!'

They made a feeble gesture of pursuit, but quickly gave up, deciding that, whatever happened, here was something that sooner or later would come their way.

'Damn you!' swore Martin, and stumbled on, while the two lawyers fell into a drunken dispute over the division of the clients.

Abruptly the streets were left behind as the frantically running figures plunged into the great yard that adjoined Timber Wharf and the river. Ahead reared the masts of moored vessels, making long black crosses against the night sky, and the smell of unseasoned wood filled the air.

Here wood was stacked in planks and poles, forming a dark geometry of passages, thin as coffins.

Martin glimpsed the white mask glimmering and grinning at him round a corner; then it vanished and he pursued. Again he saw it – and the grin seemed wider and the teeth more pronounced. He ran towards it, but it darted out of sight and the wooden corridor was empty.

Once he met it almost face to face, down a long perspective between two walls of planks. It hopped and scampered on incredibly thin legs, seemed to try and scale the wall, then darted off into another part of the maze.

Suddenly Martin felt that the figure was taunting him, was playing with him and that the death's-head grin concealed a grin even more malevolent. So he grew cunning, conserving his strength and even pausing in a black angle. Sure enough, the whitely grinning mask poked out – and Martin shouted and rushed. But even so, he lost him. Then there was silence everywhere, as if both pursuer and pursued were playing at the same piece of cunning and standing on the edge of corners.

Martin began to creep stealthily along first one passage and then another until, without any warning, the maze ended. Before him stretched an open space of cobbles, extending towards a low parapet. He could hear the river grunting and rushing below. Standing against the parapet, glaring and grinning at him, was the man in the carnival mask.

Slowly and fearfully Martin approached. He had the

feeling that any sudden movement or cry of his would cause the figure to vanish, or fly away, or even to plunge into the river below.

The death's head grinned and seemed to confirm Martin in his fear.

'Will you come with me . . . now?' asked Martin, with profound gentleness. He had halted perhaps seven or eight feet away. The figure did not move.

'I know what you have done,' went on Martin, still not daring to raise his voice or depart from an almost inaudible softness. 'You must come with me . . . It is necessary, you know. It must be done.'

The death's head nodded, but with an unrepentant grin.

'Will you take off your mask? Sooner or later I must see your face. You cannot hide it for ever . . .'

Again the death's head nodded, and, removing the mask, revealed a face not altogether dissimilar.

'I'm surprised that you did not know me before,' said Dr Dormann, flexing his lips over his awkward teeth.

'No! No! No!' groaned Martin, and covered his face with his shaking hands. Suddenly everything had collapsed in ruins about him. He felt the utter impossibility of defeating this man. Wherever he turned, however he tried, even in the recesses of his own mind, this man always rose up before him, blasting him with an inexplicable hatred. More than ever he found himself returning to his strange fantasy, that everything – sky, stars, the green world with all its men and women – was painted on a curtain that drew aside to reveal the pale, peering face of Dr Dormann. He felt himself reaching out, as if to find the joining of this curtain in order to tear it down.

'Where – where is the other . . . the man who committed the crime? What have you done with him?'

'You are quite mistaken in that, Mr Young! Do you

know, I almost called you Martin? I realize it would be an unpardonable familiarity, but I feel I know you so well. But as I was saying, you are quite mistaken! I think you must have been led astray! No, no! I didn't mean to refer to our little run together! I meant that there *is* no other man. Not now. It's all over. You noticed the fire, I suppose . . . the burning fiery furnace? I don't really have to tell you what it was that was being consumed to ashes. Yellow stars, eh? So you can see that what was, no longer is . . . to put it in the style of language I used to be fond of in my student days. The crime, Mr Young, still sits closest to you and to – yours.'

'*Damn you!*'

'Yes, yes. You had to say that. But won't you accept defeat with a good grace? You *are* in a state of grace, I suppose? But that's not a question I have any right to ask! You love – and that's grace. Do you know which is the holiest book in the scripture? The Song of Songs! That's absolutely true. A learned man – Rabbi Akiba – called it the holiest of holies. So you see that, if you consent now to pay me – pay the garden, that is – to keep the secret, then you will be paying for love and great holiness. There can be no shame in that!'

Martin bowed his head.

'Why do you hate me?' he whispered. 'Why have you destroyed me?'

'Hate . . . destroy?' stammered Dr Dormann, confused by the directness of the question. 'Because – because . . .'

Although Martin had not moved, he began to back away until he was forced to mount the parapet as if he'd been threatened with actual violence. 'I – I have to look after the garden,' he went on, abandoning his previous beginning. 'I only represent the garden . . . and Mrs Bray. I do everything for her –'

'You've done well, Dr Dormann. She should be very grateful to you.'

'She will! She will!' cried Dr Dormann ecstatically. 'She –' He stopped. A confused expression of fear and rage came over his face.

'Get away! Get away from here!'

A third figure had joined them; a man, squat, broad-shouldered and also masked, but like a nightmare.

'Sir – sir! Oh what a job I had finding you! But I could hear your friend shouting . . . that was lucky! I wanted to tell you that I burned it . . . you know what! It's all gone!'

'Get away!'

'I wanted to tell you . . . I forgot before, but I think it's important. There was a hat he was wearing! That's why I never knew. And the dress. I tore it off him and wore it to go out of the garden. It's important, that . . .'

'Go – go!' screamed out Dr Dormann; but the flood-gates of confession he'd opened could not be closed, and the tide came gabbling, panting and rushing through. The wretched man, bemused with relief and seeking again to experience the divine ecstasy of unburdening himself, confessed his crime to the sky, the stars, the dark wharf, and to Martin Young. He couldn't help himself; he was like one drunk . . .

Dr Dormann, swaying on the parapet, saw Martin begin to smile, to laugh at this sudden turn of his fortune. His enemy looked transfigured with joy.

Dr Dormann closed his eyes. He had lost everything. The nightmare he himself had unleashed had overtaken him. He had failed. The huge woman he served would have no mercy. It was not in her nature to be merciful; and he would not have wanted her to be. What was it she said? Ah yes. 'You'll be the one who goes to hell.' She was a great wise woman. She had even warned him that the blood on the ledger page was his own.

'We must accept defeat,' he muttered, when the nightmarish voice of confession was momentarily stilled to draw breath, 'with a good grace. So . . . so go now, and leave me alone. Go back – go back to the woman. Go back to your books and – and your church. Go back there, Mr Young! I understand such things . . . I was a student myself, you know. Oh! The things I used to read! And the wonderful things I found . . . and lost! Do you know, I could never remember? That's the really important thing! To have a good memory. To find . . . and to keep, in the head! Not to lose anything . . . Oh yes, I read a great deal, sir –'

'That's true!' broke in the nightmare enthusiastically. 'He's a wonderful man! Disputing with the doctors, he told me. In and out of all the churches and chapels and synagogues! Can you be surprised that he was able to help me?'

'What is it? What is it, man?' cried Martin suddenly. Dr Dormann had begun to clutch and scratch at his face as if the skin had become a mass of unbearable irritation.

'I told you – before – that I was a – a sufferer . . .'

Martin moved a pace towards him, feeling that the victory was more difficult to endure than the defeat. His heart ached for this wicked, devilish man . . .

'My face! My face!' screamed Dr Dormann suddenly. 'It's killing me!'

'Come back! Come back!' shouted Martin, and threw himself forward to save the toppling, falling figure. He held him and, for a moment, the two men seemed to be struggling on the edge of the parapet. Then, with a terrible cry, they both plunged down, still fiercely in each other's arms, and crashed into the dark, rushing river.

*

The foregoing accident was witnessed by a sailor on a vessel tied up at Timber Wharf. He gave the alarm and watermen came as quickly as they could; but despite the most energetic searches, only one of the two who had fallen was recovered ... and then only by strenuous and even brutal efforts. The man in the water fought quite desperately against rescue, shouting that he must save his companion, who, in the waterman's opinion, must have been as dear to him as a brother. He had to tap him on the head with an oar and stun him before it was possible to haul him into the boat.

No trace of the other was found, either during that night or on the next day. But, as the tide was high and on the turn, the river was running swiftly, so it was possible that he had been swept away. Several days later a body was recovered by Shadwell, but it was so battered by its progress that it was unrecognizable; as someone said, it looked like it had been through a mangle.

It might have been the body of the other man, but no one came forward either to identify it or even to report such a man's loss. It would seem that he had not been much missed.

But by far the strangest feature of the whole occurrence was the discovery, on the parapet by Dorset Stairs, from where the two men had been seen to fall, of a man in a carnival mask sitting and weeping that a saint, an angel had gone to his death.

When he was led away, he kept pleading and even demanding the right to confess. Naturally it was supposed, at first, that he wanted to take on himself the blame for the accident, although the sailor, who had seen the whole thing, was adamant that the two men had seemed to plunge in of their own accord. But it turned out that the man was insisting on admitting to something of a much graver nature. He wanted to confess to the murder of the staymaker's apprentice in the Mulberry Pleasure Garden in Clerkenwell.

Subsequently, when the reliability of his confession was established beyond doubt – by the possession of various articles of clothing partly consumed by fire, and the ownership of the knife – he was committed to prison and tried for the crime. However, in view of the circumstances, the charge was mitigated from murder to justifiable homicide and he left the court, technically a free man.

Chapter Twenty-two

'THE cure was more savage than the condition,' said the surgeon who attended Martin after he was taken from the river and carried back to his house. 'He has suffered a severe concussion of the brain. I think he will recover his life, but for his reason I cannot answer. When he returns to consciousness, you must prepare yourselves for a different man. His delirium is not the result of a fever. There *is* no fever. It is the consequence of a bruising of the substance of the brain, setting up an irritation that communicates itself to the limbs, causing them to jerk and thrash about. If he is not to do himself further injury in this state, it would be better to secure his wrists and ankles to the ends of his bed by means of padded straps. Otherwise, I fear, you will have not only an idiot but a cripple on your hands.'

'He is wrastlin' wi' the de'il,' said Mrs Jackson. 'And I willna tie him down and gie the de'il sich an advantage over him!'

The surgeon appealed to Martin's mother; but Mrs Young, who had come directly and was staying with her friends in Hanover Square, whatever her feelings, was no match for the fiercely possessive Scotchwoman. After the feeblest of protests on behalf of the surgeon, she gave up with the reflection that Jackson was, after all, an experienced nurse. Besides, to have carried her point she would have needed to remain at Martin's bedside, and this she could not do. The sight of her once-radiant son, struggling and raging and screaming, and kicking off all his coverings, distressed her beyond measure; she dreaded going in to see him, and she only did it because she knew it was her duty.

During this time, many people called and left cards with messages of sympathy and concern, while for the humbler parishioners Mrs Jackson provided a book in which their names were inscribed so that the master might thank them with the words of his own lips. Fanny Bush's name was recorded on every page.

'It's no gude your trying to see him, lassie,' explained Mrs Jackson to the girl who haunted the vicarage like a pretty moth. 'He dinna ken his ain mother.'

Then she went back to the sufferer, covered him up and seated herself by his head to watch over the spasms and contortions that passed across his features and never seemed to cease.

'That's right, master! You're fighting the gude fight! It's a great battle ... even like that of St David of Banchory when he struggled for twa days and nights before he prevailed and cast the Enemy doon into the Dee. I can see it's fierce, but wi' God's help, you'll prevail!'

And, weighing in on the side of the angels, she wiped away the saliva and sweat and forced as much beef broth between Martin's clenched teeth as she dared, without choking him.

To Martin himself, these intrusions of nourishment were an unbearable interruption. Although it was true that the violent jerkings of his limbs, his frequent shoutings-out and the expressions of intense effort that flickered across his face were due to the bruising of his brain from the blow of the waterman's oar, it was equally true that they reflected the energy of a battle he was waging on a scale that his waking mind could never have tolerated.

Mostly this battle, which consisted of many encounters, took place on such mountain sides as the saints of his childhood had fought their mysterious fights on. Like them, he stood with legs astride and every muscle braced to withstand the onslaught of the fallen angel that crawled up towards him from the black waters below. So clear was the mountain air and so precise his vision that he could make out the veining of the angel's folded wings and marvelled how closely they resembled enormous black leaves.

Then, with a great shriek and a beating of wings, the angel-devil flew at him and his nurse cried:

'Cast him doon! Cast him doon, master!'

But this was easier said than done; for, as the being flew up, the black wings became golden in the light and the shadowed face became exquisitely beautiful.

'Dinna look upon him!'

Obediently he shut his eyes and fought, not against leathery skin and barbed limbs, but with soft, yielding things, like pillows and gentle flesh.

'You're hurting me! You're hurting me!' wept and whimpered the golden angel.

'Dinna listen, master! Dinna listen!'

So he shut the sound out of his ears and wrestled on, even though his heart had gone out of the struggle. What he was doing seemed such an enormous pity . . .

'Dinna think, master! Dinna feel! Only fight the gude fight!'

'I'm sorry . . . so sorry!' groaned Martin, and thrust with all his might till he and the angel, locked in each other's arms, went flying down the mountain side into the black river below.

This was but one of his dreams; there were many others, and, although the locality and antagonist of his battle changed – sometimes he was poised on the rotunda of the Mulberry Garden, and sometimes at the edge of the lake pit, wrestling with Sir David Brown, or the blind beggar or even the child Briskitt – there always came that sense of aching dismay at the moment of victory, which, in the way of dreams that take part of their substance, like sign-posts, from the waking world, always coincided with Mrs Jackson's administrations of beef broth. The liquid ran over his tongue like vinegar.

It was curious also that not once did he dream of wrestling with Dr Dormann. The truth of the matter was, that he couldn't remember what Dr Dormann looked like.

Then, little by little, these dreams became lighter and less substantial. Details became blurred and suffused with a pervasive radiance. They resembled patterns on a gauze curtain through which he could just discern great shapes moving to and fro. Presently he distinguished the face and form of his nurse, smiling at him with worn, red eyes.

'Ye've done it, master! You've cast him doon!'

'What day is it? How – how long have I been . . . here?'

'It's Wednesday, master. Ye've been lying here since the Friday night.'

He closed his eyes, unable to comprehend any more. When his mother called, he was asleep.

On the next day, his recovery was beyond doubt. He was able to sit up and he displayed every sign of compre-hension and intelligence. Excepting an indefinable melan-choly that hovered at the back of his eyes, he seemed much the man he'd been before. When told of the many well-wishers, he insisted on being brought their cards so that he might dictate answers; and he was particularly pleased with the book which Mrs Jackson had provided for those who had no cards to leave.

'So she came . . . she came,' he murmured, turning the pages with a smile.

He did not speak of the struggle on the parapet nor even ask after the man he had tried to save. The surgeon believed that this episode had been lost from his memory and would not return. The only other ill-effect the surgeon, anxious to justify his prognosis, could discover was a weakness in the left leg, not uncommon following injuries to the brain.

'He will almost certainly limp,' he said. 'He may even require a stick.'

'Ye canna,' said Mrs Jackson, 'expect a mon to cast down the de'il and come off scot-free!'

In point of fact, his memory was unimpaired and the weakness of his leg – a useless giving-way whenever he tried to put weight on it – was the only tangible consequence of his experience.

He had not asked about Dr Dormann because he knew the man was dead. This knowledge produced a sensation of the most intense melancholy he had ever experienced; it was a sorrow for something done that was made immeasurably deeper by his being unable to wish it undone. Mrs Jackson had spoken truly when she'd said a man does not cast down the devil and come off scot-free.

He limped to the window from where he could see, above the intervening roof-tops of dark tenements, alehouses and a part of the prison, the tufted trees of the Mulberry Garden. They seemed to be building something there; a wooden tower of scaffolding had sprung up, as if from a magic seed.

As he leaned against the sill, staring towards the garden, a host of thoughts and feelings came crowding upon him, like dogs for the bones of a feast. Briskitt shivering in the pit, and the old wretch from Hatton Garden, shivering in his cold stone house; the murderer, abject and trembling

to confess, no matter what it cost, and Dr Dormann himself, screaming out that his face was killing him.

As they'd fallen from the parapet, they'd been so close
together that Martin's face had touched against the other
man's. His skin had been as cold as ice and had rasped
like rough wood.

He shook his head and turned away from the window.
Warmth: that was all that mattered in the end . . .

Chapter Twenty-three

'It's the lassie, master. Will ye see her for a wee while?'

It was late; almost nine o'clock on the Friday evening. Many visitors had managed to come before. His mother in the morning, full of cheerful gossip, begging him to come down to the country for the air, and moving about the room, tidying this and that and never staying still for a moment, as if pursued by a vague shadow of guilt. Then others, smiling, expressing in a rush their pleasure on seeing him recovered, fidgeting awkwardly and plainly eager to make their escape, having spent themselves in the first moments and been left with nothing more to say.

But why had she left it so late? Everyone else had managed earlier . . .

'She says her Mrs Gish wouldna let her out before as she had work to finish,' said Mrs Jackson, in answer to Martin's unspoken question. 'I told her it was late and you were tired fra visiting; but it seemed a shame as the puir lassie has made herself look so bonny, and she's brought ye a present, as well, master. I hadna the heart to turn her awa'.'

Mrs Jackson, in spite of her superstitions and warlike army of fictitious saints, was an admirable Christian. Whenever it was in her power, she did what she could to assist the fulfilment of the prophecy that the poor, the meek and the humble should inherit the earth. Far from insisting on her master's social standing, she would sooner have kept the Bishop from seeing him than Fanny Bush, who had washed and dressed herself so prettily and, most likely, had not two pennies to bless herself. Martin's mother knew this and resented it bitterly; she put it down to Jackson's getting her own back for being dismissed. But she was wrong. Whatever else there was about Mrs Jackson that was out of place, it was certainly not her heart. She really did believe that the meek and the humble were the children of God.

She went away to fetch Fanny Bush, and Martin hoped that she'd not noticed that he, too, had been at some pains to make himself bonny for the visitor he'd looked for every minute of the long day.

'Here's the lassie,' said Mrs Jackson; and at once the room was filled with the savour and perfume of Fanny Bush's femininity as she came in, resplendent in her white dress with the little red flowers, and crowned with a bonnet of straw.

She smiled broadly at Martin, then faltered, looked concerned, even a little dismayed, as he limped heavily towards her.

'I didn't know –' she began.

'That I'm lame?' finished Martin. 'It's nothing, really. Mrs Jackson tells me I look quite distinguished with a stick. A soldier back from foreign wars.'

'I told him,' said Mrs Jackson, observing the lassie to tremble with nervousness, 'that ye had a wee present for him.'

She nodded with every encouragement, and remained in the doorway. Although it was uppermost in her mind to be helpful, she was also inquisitive to see what was in the wee parcel the lassie clutched in her hand so fiercely.

It turned out to be a cambric handkerchief, finely embroidered round the hem, with a large M and Y stitched in silver thread at one corner.

'*My?*' said Martin curiously.

'It's your initials,' said Fanny uncomfortably. 'That's right, ain't it?'

'Oh yes – yes! I didn't think . . . It's very lovely. Thank you . . .'

'It's beautiful sewing,' said Mrs Jackson. 'Ye must have strained your een, lassie.'

'Oh no! It was quite easy, really!' said Fanny eagerly, and then, feeling that she might have undervalued herself, added, 'I made up the pattern out of my own head.'

'Ye have a real gift,' said Mrs Jackson, with compassion.

'It's almost too good to use,' said Martin; and Fanny felt miserably that the subject of the handkerchief had been quite exhausted.

The housekeeper had particularly asked her not to talk of anything that might excite the master, as he was still very weak; and now, seeing him pale as a sheet and lame into the bargain, she could think of nothing easy to say. She began to wish fervently that she hadn't come. The rich room, bright with wax candles, and the housekeeper beside her, made her feel shabby and hopelessly out of place.

She wanted to say that she'd waited for him last Friday till the garden had shut, and then gone home in tears of anger and fear. She wanted to tell him that the reason she'd come so late was that she'd been working her fingers to the bone (and burning Mrs Gish's best candles) to finish his present; and that the stupid mistake about the initials had only been because she'd run out of silver thread before she'd done the full stop.

But there was no doubt that any of these things would have excited him.

'It's a fine evening,' she said. 'It's warm as toast.'

Mrs Jackson sighed and agreed with her. Martin turned to look out of the window before confirming the observation.

'It's a lovely view,' said Fanny. 'You can even see the lights of the Mulberry Garden. You'll be able to watch the fireworks tonight.'

'I didn't know there was going to be a display.'

'Oh yes! There's a notice about it.'

'Then ye'll be wantin' to get along, lassie . . . or you'll miss the best places!'

'She could watch from here, Mrs Jackson,' said Martin suddenly.

'But won't the puir lassie want to go to the garden? She's bonny enough to be growing there!'

'Will you stay . . . and watch the fireworks with me?'

Fanny cast an uneasy glance at Mrs Jackson.

'If ye'll ring, master, when the lassie wants to leave, I'll come back for her.'

When the door had closed behind Mrs Jackson, Martin began to limp back towards his bed.

'Let me help you.'

'No – no, it's all right. I must get used to it.'

But Fanny ignored his protest and offered her arm, which he took gratefully and with a heart that beat so violently that Mrs Jackson would have boxed Fanny's ears and sent her packing.

He sat heavily on his bed and Fanny seated herself beside him.

'Do you . . . really like the handkerchief?'

'I told you. I think it's beautiful!'

'You haven't really looked at the pattern.'

'I would rather look at the head it came out of.'

'Please don't talk like that.'

'Why not?'

'Your housekeeper would be vexed. She said you were not to be excited.'

'Why should saying such a thing excite me?'

'Because – because it excites me.'

'Then let's be calm, Fanny. We mustn't vex Mrs Jackson. Read to me till the fireworks begin. Will you do that?'

If you want me to. What shall I read? What's that book beside you? Shall I read from that?'

'It's the Bible.'

'Oh! That *would* be coals to Newcastle!'

'Read it to me.'

'But I shouldn't. It would be wrong. I'd feel uncomfortable.'

'Here, Fanny. Read it.'

'But I'll make mistakes. I won't know how to pronounce some of the words. You'll laugh at me . . .'

'I promise not to laugh.'

'Close your eyes, then. Or look the other way. Remember what your housekeeper said. You're not to be excited. *"The Song of Songs, which is Solomon's."'*

'Someone told me, not long ago, that it is the holiest book in the Scriptures.'

'Be quiet, and listen, then. *"Let him kiss me with the kisses of his mouth: for thy love is better than wine."'*

'The Rabbi Akiba, I was told, said it was the holiest of holies.'

'*I am black but comely, O ye daughters of Jerusalem, as the tents of Kedar, as the curtains of Solomon.*'

'Some say that it is the story of a country girl, loved by the king, and she defends herself against the scorn of the court ladies; and perhaps even Solomon's mother.'

'*While the king sitteth at his table, my spikenard sendeth forth the smell thereof. A bundle of myrrh is my well-beloved unto me; he shall lie all night betwixt my breasts.*'

'According to another wise man, this refers to the Church's love for Christ. A teacher by the name of Origen. It's true, you know . . .'

'*Behold, thou art fair, my beloved, yea, pleasant: also our bed is green. I am the rose of Sharon, and the lily of the valleys . . .*'

'There speaks the sunburned country girl; the lass loved by the king.'

'*He brought me to the banqueting house . . .*'

'You see? There *is* a story!'

'*– and his banner over me was love. Stay me with flagons, comfort me with apples: for I am sick of love. His left hand is under my head, and his right hand doth embrace me.*' She paused in her reading as if awaiting a commentary; but Martin was silent.

'*My beloved is mine, and I am his: he feedeth among the lilies. Until the day break, and the shadows flee away . . .*'

The candle by which she read flickered before her breath, and her face danced in the varying light.

'*By night on my bed I sought him whom my soul loveth: I sought him but I found him not . . .*'

'But she found him. I promise you that!'

'*Thou hast ravished my heart, my sister, my spouse . . . how much better is thy love than wine . . .*'

'The king is speaking now. He speaks with two voices – for man and woman. First he's one, then the other. This is why the book is so holy. It is neither man nor woman, but both in a single voice.'

'*A garden enclosed is my sister, my spouse; a spring shut up, a fountain sealed.*'

The candles stirred and licked at their wicks, and the wax ran down in tears that turned to alabaster.

'*Awake, O north wind; and come, thou south; blow upon my garden, that the spices thereof may flow out ... Let my beloved come into his garden, and eat his pleasant fruits ...*'

'The garden. Always the garden, you see ...'

'Hush! "*I am come into my garden, my sister, my spouse; I have gathered my myrrh with my spice ... Open to me, my sister, my love ... for my head is filled with dew and my locks with the drops of the night.*"'

Faintly, from outside, came sounds of shouting and laughter, which, by their remoteness, seemed to increase the quiet in the room, like a garden enclosed.

'*I have put off my coat; how shall I put it on? I have washed my feet; how shall I defile them? My beloved put in his hand by the hole of the door, and my bowels were moved for him. I rose up to open to my beloved; and my hands dropped with myrrh, and my fingers with sweet-smelling myrrh upon the handles of the lock.*'

The sounds from the street grew louder, as if a party of apprentices and their girls, flushed with wine, were hastening bemusedly towards the firework night in the Mulberry Garden.

'*How fair and how pleasant art thou, O love, for delights! ... Set me as a seal upon thine heart, as a seal upon thine arm: for love is strong as death.*'

Someone cried out, as if she'd fallen and bruised herself against a street post. Then there was laughter again ...

'*I am my beloved's, and his desire is towards me ... Make haste, my beloved, and be thou like to a roe or to a young hart upon the mountains of spices.*'

The revellers outside, apparently having found their way, began to retreat, singing as they went.

'*I charge you, O ye daughters of Jerusalem, by the roes and by the hinds of the field, that ye stir not up, nor awake my love, till he please.*'

The room fell silent; the candle flames languished idly round their wicks and their slow-dropping tears solidified in soft, luxurious locks and braidings. Martin slept.

Outside, the party of revellers had departed; they'd found their tipsy way into the Mulberry Garden, only just in time for the grand display.

The garden was in a condition of crowded darkness; all the lanterns in the trees were out, and dim, mysterious figures, each bearing a glowing point of fire, moved to and fro under the spidery scaffolding, like fireflies in a web. These were Mr Cuper's maimed assistants, touching off the fuses . . .

Presently the fireflies retired, leaving behind them numerous small, burning eggs, laid in the interstices of the scaffold. For a moment it seemed that one of the eggs had gone out; a figure darted forward to rekindle it, then retired hastily as a violent hissing noise announced the imminence of the explosion.

Fifteen or twenty rockets went up simultaneously, forming, as it were, a forest of intolerable brightness in the sky. Tall trunks of white fire raced up, sending out bowers and arbours of brilliant leaves; then this was joined by a multitude of wheels and serpents, cascading green and red smoke through the fiery forest; then more rockets, until a gigantic frame was formed for the set-piece itself.

At last, after a full half minute of this pyrotechnic garden in the air, two huge countenances could be discerned, at first picked out faintly amid the surrounding brightness, and then increasing in fiery violence till they stood out, laughing and weeping, in a double eruption of wheels and saucissons making furnaces of stars. Comedy and Tragedy, burning and shouting in clouds of green and red.

Shouts and cries of 'Hurrah for the Mulberry Garden!' greeted this final magnificence; and all the garden was bathed in the wild, unnatural glare. The rotunda, the arbours, the walks and the colonnades lay transfigured under the furious radiance. The crowds became painted marble, and in the trees the children, the little squinting children, became transparent among the leaves.

The grandeur continued for about a minute, dispensing everywhere the bitter-sweet smell of burnt saltpetre; then, when all seemed over, came Mr Cuper's final cosmic effect.

By an ingenious arrangement of hinges, the two burning countenances appeared to peel away, as if two enormous actors were unmasking at the end of a play.

For a moment, the previous brightness lingered on the inner eye ... then blackness. The masks were all; there was nothing behind them.

A sigh, and almost a groan, came up from the watching crowd. Then, as the eye grew accustomed, Mr Cuper's intention became clear. The blackness thinned and beyond, calm and distinct, shone the stars of heaven. Here was an unmasking indeed!

A latecomer hastened along Rag Street. He was late, so late! A sturdy little man with astonishingly gentle eyes. Major Smith, clutching his pewter medallion, was panting with effort. Everything had conspired to delay him; his daughters, his wife and his maddening assistant.

Suddenly he was accosted. A blind beggar with a villainous-looking black dog.

'If you please, sir ... can you tell where I can find the gate of the Mulberry Garden? Me and my lady here seem to keep missing it.'

'Garden? Garden? What garden?' muttered Major Smith, dropping a coin into the beggar's extended tin. 'Oh! The old Mulberry Garden! I'm afraid it's closed down, my friend. The gate's been walled up. You're too late. You're wasting your time in these parts.'

He retreated, frowning and shaking his head. He had done his best to be tactful; he hadn't wanted to hurt the poor devil's feelings. But really! A dog in the garden? And with all those trees?

He broke into a run; and then, realizing that the sound of his footsteps would betray his direction, he crossed and recrossed the street several times before finally approaching the gate.

'Oh well!' he sighed. 'One has to protect the garden!'

He straightened his shoulders, threw out his chest, and passed inside the Mulberry Garden, leaving behind all the little plagues and miseries belonging to the woollen draper of Ludgate Hill.

With youth in his step, he strode towards the rotunda, where Orpheus Jones had begun to sing; where Tom Hastey and his Lucy stole kisses, while Lucy's aunt won a paper flower and a sugared plum; and where the lovely Leila Robinson was waiting for her widowed lover from romantic Bombay.

Somewhere outside, the blind beggar shook his bandaged old head.

'We don't believe 'im,' he grumbled to his black dog. 'It's somewhere near. We knows it, don't we! We can hear it; we can smell it . . .'

He began to tap once more along the wall.

'Some day we'll find our way in, old girl. Some day, before the winter . . .'

The black dog snarled and tugged at her string.

'Will you take me to the Mulberry Garden, sir? Point me towards the gate . . .'

But no one answered, and the sightless air was full of the sound of departing feet. Where was the garden?

Eastward in Clerkenwell lay the Mulberry Pleasure Garden: six acres of leafy walks, colonnades, pavilions and arbours of box, briar and vine, walled in between Rag Street and New Prison Walk . . . the garden of two childhoods.

Also in
Lions Tracks

To order direct from the publisher, just tick the titles you want and fill in the order form on the last page.

Lions Tracks

Also available in
Lions Tracks

The Falklands Summer *John Branfield*	£2.25
Bury the Dead *Peter Carter*	£2.50
The Chocolate War *Robert Cormier*	£2.50
The Owl Service *Alan Garner*	£2.25
The Fourth Plane at the Flypast *Dennis Hamley*	£2.25
That was Then, This is Now *S. E. Hinton*	£1.95
Slake's Limbo *Felice Holman*	£1.95
Z for Zachariah *Robert O'Brien*	£2.50
Talking in Whispers *James Watson*	£2.25
The Undertaker's Gone Bananas *Paul Zindel*	£2.25

To order direct from the publisher, just tick the titles you want and fill in the order form on the last page.

Lions Tracks

All these books are available at your local bookshop or newsagent, or can be ordered from the publishers.

To order direct from the publishers just tick the titles you want and fill in the form below:

Name _____

Address _____

_____

Send to: Collins Children's Cash Sales
           PO Box 11
           Falmouth
           Cornwall
           TR10 9EN

Please enclose a cheque or postal order or debit my Visa/Access –

   Credit card no:

   Expiry date:

   Signature:

– to the value of the cover price plus:

UK: 80p for the first book, and 20p per copy for each additional book ordered to a maximum charge of £2.00.

BFPO: 80p for the first book and 20p per copy for each additional book.

Overseas and Eire: £1.50 for the first book, £1.00 for the second book, thereafter 30p per book.

Lions Tracks reserve the right to show new retail prices on covers which may differ from those previously advertised in the text or elsewhere.

Lions Tracks